WHO KILLED KATE

A novel by

Kate Korbel

22/05/15

To Jeff & Liz

Dedication

MOTHER (Katarina Korbelova)

The most important person in my life. I would not be able to achieve what I did without your help, love and support.

SISTER (Petronela Korbelova)

Your love and friendship mean everything to me. Your encouragement made me go forward when I wasn't sure if I could continue.

Martin Pennell

It would be impossible to get this book out there without your help and great contribution to the story. Thank you and let's enjoy our accomplishment.

Prologue: Chapter 1

The time flies when you are having fun. However, I am not laughing very hard at the moment. I have been running for hours, trying to find a place to hide but I can't seem to get rid of them. How did things get so out of control so quickly? Everything was going well, professional life was fulfilling, the job was progressing and my personal life has finally started having some kind of meaning. So I must ask myself the question: What did happen? Ok, there is no time for overthinking, I really need to find a place to hide and regain my energy before I make any decisions about what to do next. I make a fast turn into the dark alley and toward a residential building. There is a guy, barely standing on his feet trying to get inside too by using chopsticks, possibly a homeless man looking for a place to sleep during this terrible New York weather. Winter in this city can be sometimes unpredictable and unbelievably cold but somehow it still manages to uphold beautiful scenery during the daytime. However, this is my chance so I start running faster towards the building. The drunken guy must hear some noise behind him and turns just in the moment that I reach the front stairs. We collide and fall together on the floor. I curse under my nose but what really worries me is the fact that the man must have broken his arm in the process and now is screaming uncontrollably. Whoever has been following me knows exactly where I am right now. I try to get up but the guy keeps gripping my long dark hair with his dirty, undamaged hand and keeps yelling at me.

'What hell you think you doing, stupid girl? Don't you see me? Now look what you did?' The man screams at me and I am now seriously starting to panic. The shadows are now no longer shadows but instead of them, I see two bulky men coming to get me and if I don't get rid of this idiot under me they might even succeed. I kick the guy in the groin and quickly stand up and run into the building, not looking back. It takes me couple of minutes before I become aware of the fact that I am lost but that doesn't stop me and I continue running up the stairs till I reach the roof. The roof is deserted, which is expected this time of the day. There are couple of empty chairs which means that people like to occasionally find their way up to admire the beautiful view; the Statue of Liberty that is slightly visible through another block of buildings on the left side. I move closer to the edge and see some people walking the street, unaware that my life is now coming to the end. I just wish that I could wake up and find out that this is just a nightmare and nothing more but I know that this wish will not come true. My hairs are gently caressed by the ice-cold wind as I am contemplating my next move. Suddenly, there is a strong noise behind me and a chill runs down my whole spine. This time weather has nothing to do with my feeling of dread. I turn around and see a group of men that look as they went through whole Spartacus boot-camp at least three times. Some of them were pointing guns at me and the rest of them were just watching the spectacle. I get mentally ready for the fight even though my body is telling me that I can try but I still will not be able to win. There is no move from them. It looks as they are waiting for something. I strongly hope it is not me begging as that will never happen. I will rather go to hell than to give them satisfaction like that.

'You know what I want, KATE SUMMERS, if that is your real name of course. Don't make me to ask again.' The figure appears from behind one of the bodyguard. It is the BOSS of the organisation. I feel privileged that he felt the need to be personally present but then I do deserve all the attention that I can get for what I did. Now I know it is serious and I am possibly looking at the death penalty. I can't let them know that I am anxious to know what is coming but instead I look as confident as possible. I cannot give in even if the outcome would be my ultimate end.

Chapter 2

The BOSS is not somebody that likes to wait for someone's obedience. He is used to everybody following all his commands. Impatience could be seen in his old, wrinkled face that still looks quite young considering that he just turned sixty a couple of weeks ago. The age and his Mexican nationality are the only things that you are able to find out about this man. I have been trying to dig up as much background information about him as possible in order to prepare for my assignment but the man is a chameleon and knows how to cover his tracks. I wasn't even able to find out his real name so I decided to call him, as everybody else did, 'the boss'.

'I have no idea how I could be of the service to you anymore. I told you everything I know.' I try my best to remain calm and maybe hopefully get out of it with just couple of broken bones.

'Do you think that my age is getting to me, Kate? Don't underestimate me. I know that you are a traitor and now I just need to know what you told them so let's not make this situation too bloody.' He smiles at me without sincerity. I look around and try to see if there is any way I can run but it looks like only possible path for me leads steeply down the building. The boss sharply grasps the person next to him and angrily pushes him toward me.

'Make her to talk if you want to live. You two seem to be getting along well.' He snarls. A youthful looking man in expensive, dark suit put his gun higher and points it at my face as he come closer. I feel as if something kicked me in the stomach and I find it very difficult to breath. MARSHALL, the love of my life and the only person that I didn't want to see today, is standing directly in front of me. His eyes are the colour of summer grass and even the darkness of the day cannot cover his expression of despair. I cannot believe that I am the person that injected him with this pain and for a while we both feel each other's sadness. As he comes closer I cannot help myself and admire his confident demeanour and flawless appearance even in the situation such as this one. He always says that it is crucial to look strong in order for others to respect him. He joined the organisation when he was only twenty-two years old with the belief that the appearance and confident demeanour is the key to success. Even now when I look at him I can imagine his morning ritual that consisted of a heavy workout and long shower that I occasionally shared with him. My heartbeat increased the more I remember details of those mornings. He touches my face as he comes even closer, if possible.

'Kate, honey, we just need to know. One way or the other, you need to tell us the truth.'

I would love to tell him everything that I know right here, right now and as I am just about to let him know, my Intel something flashes in front of me, something that I just can't ignore. And as quickly as my weak moment came to light it also disappeared and was replaced by my strong, unreadable expression. I cannot stand the touch anymore so I turn my face away. I know that this move hurt him and possibly it could destroy everything that was between us. Everybody thinks that I betrayed them and the fact that now I am standing here and refusing to cooperate is confirming their suspicion. Dishonesty is something that Marshall will never tolerate in his life. However, the game needs to continue and everybody has to be on board so I need to stand my ground. I look back at him with renewed confidence.

'I am not sure why you are asking me the same questions again. It seems like you already made your decision anyway. So let's just get over it.'

There is a dead silence as everybody is trying to figure out if this is still some kind of game. Marshall keeps staring at me without even blinking, his eyes revealing his worry that he might miss a signal of fear that he could use against me.

'We saw...'

I quickly stop his statement, not willing to get into further details of what happened. I don't want to reveal more than is necessary by mistake.

'You think you know what you saw but you know nothing. Don't you remember that you have been wrong before?'

I have a slight glint in my eyes that makes Marshall to grin back at me, understanding the meaning behind it. The first time that we met a year ago Marshall was insisting that women cannot join the gang. He thought that women are too weak and sensitive to be able to lead and follow very demanding and sometimes difficult orders. Of course, I had proven him wrong on and then some. I was a more than capable leader and even less sensitive than men when the situation called for it.

'Either she proves us how incredibly wrong we have got it or she will take a long swan dive,' Boss barked, getting tired of my exchange with one of his best men. The moment he sees the fear in my eyes that he was waiting for, he adds with a childlike voice:

'Of course, after we shoot her. We were not brought up in the zoo.'

The men get ready and aim all their hand guns at me. Marshall's protectiveness kicks in and he stands up in front of me and holds his both hands up.

'Come on guys, let's not make any rushed decisions here. We should give her chance to....'

Marshall has always been very naïve and believed that people are generally good but sometimes circumstances force them to do things that are not so pretty. I see his weakness as my way out and grasp his belt, quickly bringing his body close to mine. I take the gun behind that Marshall left unprotected and bring it up to his left temple. My petite figure is now completely covered by Marshall's body. Everybody moves a bit backwards and freezes, surprised how quickly the whole scenario changed.

'You are not listening to me,' I say loud enough for everybody present to hear me. Marshall tries to turn his head to me but I push the gun stronger against his head, preventing his movement.

'And now you are making me to do stupid things like this.' Everybody keeps looking at each other, unsure of what to do. I see it as a chance to say something in my defence.

'I am not a mole and I didn't betray you.' Boss tilts

his head to the left while trying to comprehend what my motives are.

'A mole or a rat. Who cares what you call it. The important thing is that we all know that there is one here, right now.' Don't think that I thought for a second that they will believe me; there is too many evidence implicating me but it's still worth a try. It looks like there is no other option for me than to fight.

'I really didn't want things to go this way.'

The wait is over and the time to act is upon us. I look around and with a quick motion I push Marshall out of the way and I jump to the floor on the opposite side, taking cover as everybody start the firing. I fire back with a vengeance, taking down three people in couple of seconds. There is a wall on the opposite side of the roof that divides the one side of the building from another. There is a chance that I will find an exit ladder over there which would get me to the ground. I keep firing my ammunition on anything and everything that is moving as I start running. Suddenly sirens are heard just below us and stairways doors are flung open. Law enforcement officers rush onto the scene yelling orders to everybody. The boss aims his gun at them and starts viciously firing all his ammo hoping it will give his crew a chance to escape.

The police reciprocate and start diving for cover while the gang rushes off of the roof and away from the violent scene. There is too much motion around and not enough time to catch everybody but it is obvious that law has an upper hand in this match. I am forced to look around with bewilderment as people that I work for many years are falling down in pain or dead. I lie down on the floor avoiding the bullets when all of a sudden I sense someone else's presence behind me.

'Come on Kate, we have to get out of here!' I can't hide my surprise, seeing Marshall trying to help me out. I just tried to kill the man but he is still on my side. Meanwhile, more people are being killed around us, the majority of them belong to the low rank gang. The bigger fish are either dead or have already disappeared. I look back at Marshall with despair. However much I would love to go with him I have to stop this madness. It was supposed to be a simple ride to arrest Boss and Intel from him about organisation's plans but now Boss is lying dead on the concrete and rest of the people are being killed without warning. It is a bloodbath.

'Marshall, look at me. I cannot leave but you can.' I can see that my suggestion only made him angrier. Again, I am defying him.

'What the fuck is wrong with you woman! Why can't you listen to me for ..' I grasp his collar in the hope of shutting him up before anybody notices us. Quickly, I cover his mouth with mine. The moment that lasts only couple of seconds feels like eternity for both of us. Abruptly, I shove him aside and stand up. I slowly move towards the officers with my hands above my head, just like we were taught in the academy. This unexpected move also gives Marshall and others chance to escape.

'Don't shoot!' Once I am sure that I have their attention I get down to the floor with her arms behind my head. There are more orders being shouted my direction but my concentration is compromised as one of the officers that I haven't seen behind pushes me on the floor face down as he secures my hand.

That gives me a view towards the last spot that Marshall was hiding, a place that is now empty. Hopefully, he will use this chance and turn his life around. It hurts me immensely to know that he might go through the rest of his life hating me. I wish I could have couple of minutes with him alone so I can tell him the whole story that maybe he would understand. Maybe...

Chapter 3

It has been hours since I've been waiting in the cold, handcuffed. What the hell is taking so long to process the scene? It is not like something unique just happened. The war between drug dealers and underworld has been going on for years. Thus, this whole incident should be just a formality. I do admit that this position with my front against the car is not very comfortable; after a while when your legs start giving in. Finally, I can comprehend why guys from the precinct always laugh when they force wounded prisoners to stand like that for hours. It can be quite self-degrading. I look left with my head and see that all the officers that were just staring at my ass and giggling are now tense. They look almost as uncomfortable as I feel.

I try to look behind me to see what the fuss is about. The black undercover police car stops a couple of feet from me which made me jump in fear. I cannot see who is in there but I have quite good idea who it is so instead of trying to get a peek at him I brace myself for the inevitable fight. A hand touches my shoulder and sharply turns me around. A tall man wearing black suit and dark blue tie is standing in front of me. KEVIN COLLINS is a man that gives a strong vibe of confidence and bravery. I know that very well as I used to work with him for years. We were partners since I joined the gang investigation unit in San Jose but he has been around longer than that and now, after five years of waiting he got a chance to show off his skills by leading this investigation. Kevin's expression grows colder as he moves his body closer to me. Don't take me wrong, he is very handsome man but this close proximity makes me extremely uncomfortable. Kevin gives me a winning smile and even in the situation like this he trying to flirt with me by touching my cheek with the back of his hand. Kevin always goes around as he is some kind of gift to every woman who encounters him. He has the body that men work for every day in the gym, his own flat, no commitments and even though he is almost thirty-five he looks like he is just couple of years older than me. Many times people would think we are something more than platonic partners but I never gave him satisfaction or any indication that I might be even slightly interested. However, today is the day when I see Kevin as somebody to be scared of. He is charming but in a malicious way and I know the storm is coming. He was working on this case for months and it will not look good on his resume once his boss find out that many of the scumbags managed to escape due to my warning shot.

'Talk to me,' Kevin asks me gently. 'Come on Kate. I can only give you one chance. You have it now. Either you tell me what I want to know or it is all over.'

I want to say to him everything but I know that there would be price to pay if I do so. I shake my head with regret and slowly fall back into my unreadable and uncaring attitude. Kevin sees the chance and sighs sadly. He slowly looks to the ground. I know that he is struggling with how to deal with this situation. His next move was very surprising for everybody who has been watching us. He punched me strongly across my right side of face. The impact is so strong that I fall to the ground, almost losing my consciousness. I feel a good amount of blood pouring from my mouth and there is a possibility that I might become toothless as well. His attack didn't finish with this one punch and suddenly he starts kicking me all around my body. I never saw this side of Kevin. He was always so nice and caring towards his colleagues. During interrogation he was always considered good cop and I was the bad cop. Thus, you can imagine that this action is completely out of the character for him. I move my legs towards my torso trying to protect as much of my body as possible but the kick in the head ended my struggle and the only thing that I remember is darkness.

#

Slowly I open my eyes trying to figure out my location. The last memory that I have is of Kevin asking me questions and then viciously attacking me. That means this is heaven, hell, hospital or prison. Since I don't see anything heavenly or deadly around me I am only left with prison or hospital. The beeping machine next to me is a good indication that this must be the emergency room. I try to sit down but my hands don't seem to follow my order. Not because I am numb but because I am handcuffed to the bedposts. My condition will not allow me to do anything else than to lie back down and wait. I look around and see that I am only person in the room even though there is enough room for two other beds. Never knew that becoming criminal will give me such a huge privilege of privacy. I remember during my time in college I had to fight to get at least five minutes in the bathroom without anybody trying to barge in.

An overweight man comes into my room, looking

bored as if he was forced to be there. He sits on the chair by the door and takes a pen from his suit pocket. He holds the file in his hands and slowly goes through it while he addresses me unemotionally.

'I am attorney that was appointed to you by the state. I heard that you don't want to say anything in your defence. Is that still true?'

I nod my head weakly but without any hesitation. The attorney writes some notes down and sharply closes the folder as he looks back at me. I can see in his eyes that I am nothing more to him that another case that has no possibility to be won in the court of law.

'Well then this is as far as we go with our relationship. I have good and bad news for you. As you don't want say anything that would reduce or acquit you of charges you will definitely go to prison for some time. However, as there is not a lot of evidence against you the maximum that you can get is five years. Means you can still start over once you are released. Hopefully, the time will give you a chance to think about your actions.'

He stands up to leave but before he closes the door behind him he looks back at me and his last couple of words were the only ones that sounded sincere and human instead of meaningless speech taken from the law jargon.

'Such a shame. There are so many dirty people responsible for what happened and you will pay for their crimes. Hope it is all worth it for you.'

The door closes with a bang and silence envelopes the room as I contemplate what just happened. My only chance of being released just left the room without even properly introducing himself and the only thing that got stuck in my mind is if it was worth it. There is no simple answer to that and only time will tell if my decision was the right one.

Chapter 4: 5 YEARS LATER

I lie on the top bunk of my cell, staring at the ceiling and listening to my CELLMATE's irritating snoring. Thanks God I am leaving this hell-hole. Five years of listening to that noise every night made me want to either kill myself or kill her even for the price of extending my time here. I turn to the side and look down at the redheaded woman below. The only thing that was sticking out from under the blanket was her tattooed arm. Who would in their right mind get such an ugly ink to be permanently imprinted into their skin? I can understand if tattoo has some sentimental or religious meaning depending on the size of it but why would a fifty-year-old woman with two children, a grandchild and two divorces behind her get the tattoo of dead bird on her arm and other dead creatures all over her body is beyond me. Like she doesn't have any other disgusting traits already. I swiftly took the pillow from underneath and throw it at her hoping for some time of peace. However, the impact only made her slightly moan and turn to another side. Annoyed, I swear under my breath. This place is slowly making me crazy. Everybody here has some hidden agenda, the food stinks, the gym is always packed by lesbian butch women that are looking at themselves in the mirror while they are pumping the iron so the only thing left here to enjoy is night time. But no, I have to be stuck with the loudest snoring grandma that can be found in this godforsaken place. I put my head down on now-pillowless bed, ready to start screaming. Suddenly the door to the cell noisily open and the GUARDWOMAN points at me.

'Come with me. The councillor wants to see you before you leave.'

I jump down the bed with excitement and offer both hands to the guard in order to get handcuffs on.

'God bless you for taking me away. I was worried that if I stay here one minute my next action can lead to more years spent in here.' The guard laugh as she leads me away. If she only knew that I was telling the truth. One more second and I would jump down from the bed and show that snoring cow how to keep her mouth shut.

We move without stopping and in couple of minutes we are in front of the COUNSELLOR's door. The guard knocks on the door and wait for permission to come in. The door opens and I am greeted by the only person that I could consider a friend in this place. I didn't try to find any new pals during my time here. I am sure that not everybody here is a bad person. Sometimes circumstances force people to do things which are unexplainable but I still wanted to stay as far away from them as possible. No reason to get into any more unpredictable and possibly dangerous relationships. I don't even know who the guard that walked me here is. She seems like a nice person, very young for this kind of job but it looks like she really likes her position due to the fact that I have seen her around almost every day. There are just two reasons for it here; either she is very short of money or like to boss us around. Councillor smiles at me and with a hand motion invites me in. She closes the door behind me leaving the guard behind. The office is still dark as sun is still below horizon but through the dim light it is visible that the councillor has spent her evening going through the uncountable amount of folders that are spread around her desk and floor. That would explain the messy hair and wrinkled, grey t-shirt on the person that is usually presented very neatly. CAROLINE MOLLINS has been counselling me since I came here and after couple of sessions we realised that we have more in common that we thought was possible between criminal and law-abiding citizen. Caroline is almost forty-seven years old which makes her to be older than my own mother and twenty years older than me. We both started working in the enforcement to make a change. She has almost no contact with her family, same as me and we both mostly live for our work. Of course, she doesn't know the reason why I turned my back on my beliefs but she is pretty sure that I am hiding something. Unfortunately, even though I am certain I can trust her, there is no way I would tell her the whole story. The complete trust can be sometimes more deadly than the fastest bullet.

'Caroline, what did I tell you about living in this place. You need some vitamin D.' She laughs. I always liked to make her smile. It suits her more than always being expressionless and cautious. It makes her face light up which in turn makes her eyes brighter Now if she just fix her dark hair that reached her shoulder she would be a sight that every man would enjoying spending the rest of their day looking at.

'I think time had come for you to show me how it is done.' Caroline picks up my folder and opens it. Such a shame she spends so much time reading all this, full of lies.

'You look not yourself today Kate. What is the problem?' Caroline always knew when something was bothering me. An excitement of being released turned to deep anxiety. The people and the world as I knew changed and now I am expected to walk back in it without any path or training? The prison remains always same, same food, clothes, environment and the rules. The only thing that occasionally alters is prisoners.

'I feel a bit nervous, I think.' No reason to burden sweet Caroline. There is nothing more than she can do for me anymore. It is time for me to face the music and see if my action served the purpose. Who knows, maybe the world now will be more accepting towards people as me.

'But why is that? We were preparing for this moment for last five months and you are ready.' Caroline takes a can of Diet Coke from the drawer of desk and passes it to me. She knows that I am more open to sincerity once I have caffeine in my blood stream.

'Kate, you don't need me to tell you that there is nothing that you should be worry about. You will be fine out there.' I take couple of sips of my Coke and nod my head. However, the anxiety of what is coming is only increasing with every second. There are people out there who still hope that I would never see the light of the day and I am sure that once they discover that I am out I will spend most of my day running from them.

'I am more alone out there than I ever was in here. This is not going to change anytime soon.' This is the first time that I said laud what is my worse fear: loneliness. I have never been close to my mother or other member of my family. The only people that I ever cared about wish to see me dead and I have no longer a purpose in life. So what do I really have left out there?

'What about your sister? Karoline is her name, right?'

'We are very different people.' I look out of the window and see sunrise. It is really beautiful and for a moment I believe that things will be good again. I look back at my only friend and stand up. It is time to say good bye and start new chapter of my life. I

'But I would like to thank you, Councillor. I know it is your job but I want you to know that you made my stay here more bearable.' I go around the table and hug her. I can feel that she is surprised by my action but eventually she gives in and hug me back. The guard enters the room as Caroline releases me from the embrace.

'You know that I am more than just your councillor. We are friends and anytime you need something please call me - - Here.' Caroline passes me her business card but not before she writes her private phone number at the back of it.

'Thank you.' I smile and confidently move towards the guard who is ready with handcuffs. Silly prison rule states that I have to be in the restraints till the moment the gate closes behind me.

'Bye Kate. Good luck!' Caroline whispers, but I could still hear her before the next prisoner enter her office and shut the door.

Chapter 5

Now, I stand in front of the prison's gate wearing the same clothes as five years ago. The black jacket with blue jeans and grey t-shirt makes me feel indescribably dark and ordinary. I got used to the orange suit that all the women in California Women's Facility have to wear. The whole scenario makes you feel like your life continues as nothing happened. I look down at myself and can see that the clothes actually do fit me well. However, I do remember that they were slightly loose the evening of my arrest. Funny, I put on weight in the prison. Maybe all that dry food and at least an hour in the gym everyday made me to gain some more muscle. That can be handy later if things get wild. I am still clutching the business card that I got from Caroline. This little piece of paper is the only thing that I have left from the last five years. I put it in my black leather jacket's pocket and take a deep breath, enjoying for the moment the fresh air that I missed in the dark and dusty confinement. I smile when California's fresh air reaches my lungs. Amazingly, people would hope that after release from this place they would see some green scenery or at least some people moving around. However, the women's prison is built just across from Valley state building that is occupied by low-risk men inmates. It is comical that my first sight after living prison is that of gate which would lead to another prison. I don't let it to destroy my first moment and slowly I start walking on the side of dirty road leaving the town of Chowchilla behind. Maybe I will be lucky and somebody will give me a ride to San

Jose. I see some cars coming my way so I stick a thumb out hoping for a miracle. Of course, just as you see in the horror movies the only vehicle that eventually takes pity on me is a truck driven by old, unshaven and bold MAN that looks like serial killer ready to strike again. There is not a choice for me so quickly I get in with a smile and word of gratitude. Once inside I introduce myself but get no response back. Obviously, he must know that the only reason for me to be on this path is because I did the time so he makes smart decision by not revealing any private information. He asks where to and moves the truck back on the road. I use the quiet moment by looking out of the car window admiring the beautiful countryside. Amazing how people start appreciating simple things after they were forced to live without them.

'Once we are in the city can you please let me out by the coffee shop? I haven't eaten whole day and would kill for glass of coffee.' There is again no reply but I am sure that he heard me.

#

The truck stopped by the little coffee shop, QUATRO JOSEBE a couple of minutes later. I get out of the truck thanking the man but once again there is no response and truck gets back on the road. Hopefully, this rude interaction is no indication of what is coming. I walk toward a payphone in the back of the busy café. The WAITRESS rushes around the shop trying to keep its hungry patrons happy. I dial the number from the head and wait for somebody to pick it up but without success. Instead of friendly voice I am greeted by an automatic voice mail.

'Hey Karoline, it is me. You could have picked me

up today. - - Anyway just to let you know I am coming over now, so be in.'

I hang up the phone angrily and walk back to the coffee counter. Surprisingly, I still have couple of coins left in my jacket. I order a little chicken sandwich without dressing and black coffee. Minutes later I am back on the road aiming toward the Cherry Avenue located downtown. The fact that it is so close to Sorreno Street packed with the gangs worries me a lot; that is why I was hoping that Karoline would pick me up from prison. Once again my little sister forgot her priorities.

#

The entry doors are not fully closed. A little stone from the street is blocking it from locking down. I used people's carelessness and get inside the building unnoticed. The building consists of 12 floors and overall it is quite safe place to be living in. I wait for the lift to get down but it seems like it is either not working properly or little creature in the form of children make it their goal to irritate me. I get to Karoline's floor quite quickly and without hesitation I bang on the door. I wait for couple of more seconds and knock again but this time I add more force into it that result into the door opening on its own. I know that I got stronger working out almost every day but I am certain that I cannot break the door just by knocking on it. The lock must have been loosened up by somebody else. I peak inside carefully in case there is still somebody else inside waiting to attack anybody who gets in his or her way. Looking around I see cloths and papers spread around the floor. It looks as somebody was looking for something but now the question is what it was and if they found it. Broken mirror caused the floor to be dangerous place to stand on so I keep my shoes on. The red colour on the cream sofa catches my attention and for the first time I realised that Karoline is nowhere around. I touch the red colour and look at it closely. It has blood and lots of it.

'Karoline!!!!!' I keep screaming as I run around the two-bedroom flat trying to find any signs of where she can be. The master bedroom is in perfect condition which is very unusual. The bed is made up, the table's surface is clean and nothing valuable seems to be missing as a jewellery box is open and full of things worth stealing. Firstly, it means that whoever did it was trying to cover his tracks by making it look like as burglary and secondly they were after something else. However, I cannot think of one reason why would somebody care about Karoline. She was leading ordinary life, going to work as a waitress six times a week and taking care of Suzy. Oh My God.

'Suzy? Suzy, honey, are you here?' There is no answer. I aim towards the Suzy's bedroom cautiously that is interconnected with Karoline's room. The walls are covered by cartoon characters, mostly animals that played in the movie Madagascar. Suzy is now eight years old but her love for little animals is as strong as when she was only a little three-year-old. I took her dozens of times to the zoo and her little eyes always light up once she saw four-legged creatures. I take a little lion teddy bear from her bed and hold it to my chest. What happened in here and where is everybody. The bathroom was also untouched. The whole thing makes me nervous. Why would anybody come in here and destroy the living room but nothing else in the room. The only other conclusion is that there was some kind of struggle in the sitting area which resulted in the whole mess. The person responsible for it must have flee the scene but again it doesn't explain where Karoline is. I touch the towel that is on the floor to see if it is wet. There is not even a slight wetness so it means that whoever used it must thrown it there long time ago. My concentration is disrupted by the voice coming from the living room.

'Hello Mum, you will never believe where I am at the moment. I wish that you would be here with me right now. We would have so much fun.'

It is Suzy's voice. I run inside the living room in hope to find my sister and Suzy standing there but instead I find nothing but answering machine with red light on. The disappointment of finding an empty living room was replaced by relief. Suzy is the one leaving the voice mail which means that she is not in any immediate danger.

'Roger is here with us. He just got me another ice cream. This is my second one today!' I could always pick up the phone and tell her that I am her aunty. Maybe she will remember me. The message continues to be recorded without any response from me. I know this is maybe my only chance to find out where exactly she is and who is with her.

'I can't wait to see you soon. Love you mummy. Oh, Gran is here too. She would like to say something. Wait!'

My hand frozen and somehow I found myself on the floor as I hear DALENA on the other side. I didn't expect that I would hear the voice of my mother so soon. It is weird that the woman that was supposed to love me unconditionally and be there for me when I needed her is the person that is a complete stranger for me. She didn't come to visit me once when I was incarcerated, didn't write one letter or send one package. I know that after years of being neglected and ignored by her I shouldn't be surprise but that didn't make me feel any better.

'Hi dear. Hope you are enjoying some time by yourself. It was brilliant couple of weeks that we had together as you can hear from her voice and mine. We will tell you everything once we see you.'

The whole time she speaks I cannot help myself and look at the framed picture of me, Karoline and Dalena that is on the table next to the large TV.

'OK, so we will go now. Please do give us a call back once you hear this message. Roger says hi too.'

My eyes tear up. You would think that my mum turned her back to me the moment I was sentenced to go to prison but actually things were always like that in her family. Dalena was never interested in me as a mother. She cares only about Karoline. Maybe it was because she was always more like her, going from one man to another, enjoying the life to the fullest by using drugs and basically just wasting away the life. On the contrary, I wanted to become somebody and work hard to achieve it. Funny, I became a black sheep of the family by doing the right things and trying to be successful in the process. Eventually, the machine beeps and the recording stops exactly as memories of my childhood vanish in the air.

Chapter 6

Captain ADAMS stands in front of group of detectives, clearly upset. In his 50s, this is the first time that he has met a situation like this. He brushes his grey hair from his face and addresses the room with a no-nonsense attitude.

'As you all surely know, the number thirteen was reported to us last night. I hope you are aware how serious this situation is at the moment. We need to deal with it promptly.'

Adam's speech is rudely interrupted by Detective KAY's not-so-wise remark.

'Should we really? I don't think it is so serious.' Kay smiles and sit on the chair even more casually, if that is possible. 'Why are we even trying to solve this? I think we should thank whoever is doing all that. The night slayer is doing us a great favour taking those assholes from the streets.' There are the murmurs around the room as other detectives agree with him. Kay is known around the office as loud and opinionated. Sometimes he seems to be too cocky which might be because of his flawless performance in the department or the fact that he is only 30 years old but he still has managed to close more cases that any other detective done before in five years of service. That is maybe the only reason why Adams tolerates his occasional disrespect. However, today is not a suitable time for this at all. Things are getting worse by day and Adams is fed up being yelled at by his COMMANDER.

'Another bonus is that we don't even have to pay to the person for cleaning the street for us. We should just take it as a holiday time.' Kay says with amusement that is accompanied by more laughter. Adams looks at Kay annoyingly, who only challenges his look with a smirk. That angers Adams and he decides to end the whole circus by slamming his fist on the table in front of him

'That is enough! This is not a joke. People are being killed on the street by a psycho. It doesn't matter that victims are criminals. It is still against the law to slaughter people without giving them a proper chance to defend their actions.' Kay tries to interfere again but this time without success. Adams raises his hand before Kay manages to voice his opinion.

'Shut up Kay. I heard enough. Whoever is doing it knows things that are not accessible to public. We need to find the person before there is another murder.'

Kay decides to keep him mouth closed for now but unfortunately for the Captain there are more men in the room that support the Kay's opinion.

'We should just be happy that the killer is targeting scumbags otherwise we would be in the real trouble here!' The whole room starts laughing again. One person doesn't share their view, though: GINA SELBY, a detective in the mid-20s with blond, short hair and green eyes. She is a refined beauty but if you look deeper into her eyes you could see deep anguish and pain that is peaking just below the surface. Gina has been working in the San Jose Homicide Unit for only two years. It took her a long time to gain the respect of men working with her but eventually she succeeded. Her talent to see what others don't at the crime scenes played a significant role during many tough investigations. Last month was difficult for her and even though she is still too emotional to perform well on the street she still decided to come back to work after two weeks of sitting at home staring at the blank screen of television.

'Yes, you would definitely be in a real mess, right Kay?' Gina asked Kay angrily, who only look at her briefly without interest.

'Those druggies deserved what they got. The world is cleaner without them in it.'

Gina just sits up at her chair and this time her expression is darker. All her anger is aimed at Kay who is only two chairs in front of her. Animosity between them is not uncommon but today it may escalate into something more dangerous. Gina smiles politely and for a second it looks like everything might be fine. However, in a matter of seconds Gina bolts out of the chair and rushes for Kay. She reaches out and grasps his neck, trying to throttle him. A commotion breaks as fellow detectives try to hold the pair apart. Gina struggles against the arms that are holding her back and maintain her hold on Kay's neck. She moves even closer to him so he can feel her breath on his face.

'You think that you are soooo good, don't you Kay? Well, then how is it possible that the killer is still out there and after a month of investigation you still have no bloody clue who it is?' Gina makes her hold on Kay's neck even stronger. 'Maybe because you are only a pretentious ass with the small size of the brain that equal to your manhood.' Afterwards, she turns her head towards the rest of the room without releasing the now obviously-upset Kay.

'In fact the killer is smarter than all of you shits here put together.' Gina pushes her oppressor harder against the wall, trying to inflict even more discomfort if possible. The hand on her shoulder stops her further movement. Gina looks at the owner of the hand ready to give him piece of her mind too when she sees that it was Captain Adams. The hatred is slowly fading from her eyes as she becomes aware of her unprofessional behaviour. She releases Kay and takes a step back with shame. All the people in the room are now standing and waiting on what is about to happened.

'Can I have a moment of your time detective,' Adam addresses Gina unemotionally and pushes her toward the main door of the meeting room.

#

Gina walks with Captain out of the room towards his office in silence. Once inside Gina slumps down into the chair, obviously still upset about what happened. The room is full of medals indicating the successful career that Adams has had in the investigation unit for years. Everything is clean and neat and not one paper is out of place. Adams walks around Gina towards his leather chair. He slowly sits, not taking eyes from her. He knows how difficult it is when a person close to you is killed, especially if you are working in the police field. The need to use the skills learnt in the academy to avenge their death is immensely strong. However, the tools and services that we provide for public with cannot be used for our own benefits.

'I thought we have an understanding. Is it too soon?' Adam asks Gina with the hint of compassion. No need to show her that he understands her more than she can imagine. Gina needs to know where her place is and who is in charge. Otherwise, everybody in here would do how they please.

'No, Captain. I am very sorry for what happened. He just knows how to piss me off.' Gina responds quickly. The happiness of being back at work was replaced by despair. What if she is not ready to face the reality? What if her need to punish whoever is responsible for what happened to her younger brother will cloud her judgment? Adam raises an eyebrow and crosses his arms, not believing a word that Gina is saying. It is visible that she is under lots of stress and not handling it well. Her stubbornness and tough demeanour will not permit her to admit any kind of weakness. Especially not in front of her own boss.

'Are you certain? Cause if you are not it means you are lying to me, and you know how much I hate when people do that. So I am asking you again. Is it too soon?' Adam presses even harder.

Gina straightened up on the chair and answered with renewed confidence. She knows that if she gives any kind of indication of how she feels inside than she will be grounded again. That is unacceptable, especially if today's fiasco during meeting is any indication of how people feel about the killer that murder her brother. The guy who did this is smart and unpredictable. Yes, he is only killing people that are somehow connected to the drug world but that doesn't mean he shouldn't be brought to justice. Gina's little brother was not the best person in the world and he did some really terrible things but he definitely didn't deserve to die. Especially not in such a horrible and painful way. The only way how she can start feeling again is by catching person responsible for his suffering.

'No sir. I can handle it, I swear.'

Adam stands up and walks over to the window looking at the traffic below. This time of the day the streets are covered with people running from one place to another. Oblivious to the evilness and darkness around them.

'You know that this is not over.' Adam pauses to make sure that his words were understood. Gina knows what he is talking about. What happened in the meeting room is only one incident and there will be many more happening in the future.

'You need to find a way to keep a hold on your emotions. I cannot tolerate this kind of behaviour for too long. Are we clear?' Adam finally adds.

'Yes sir, it will not happen ever again,' Gina responds and stands up as there is a knock on the door.

'Don't give me promises that you might not be able to keep. It will only make me angrier if you don't fulfil them. - - Come in!' Adam yells out.

Kevin Collins enters the room confidently. Five years older but still looking same, handsome, tall and self-assured. His hair is shorter than before and neatly combed.

'Yes, sir you wanted to see me?'

'Please take Detective Selby to her new desk. We had to move her during her absence, as you know.' Adam looks at Gina and gives her a nod which is indication that conversation is now over and she should follow him.

#

Gina and Kevin walks through the police's corridors. Kevin walks in front her hoping to avoid any kind of conversation that he might not be able to finish. Gina speeds up her steps.

'Are there any new updates or leads?' Gina asked breathlessly. Her shorter height makes it difficult to keep up with him. Kevin turns to right as a couple of officers passed him on the corridor. He opens the door towards the staircase and lets Gina through.

'You know that I cannot talk to you about it. It wouldn't be right.' Kevin replies with regret.

They walk together to the third floor in comfortable silence. Gina is in deep thought so she doesn't even acknowledge fellow officers passing them. Kevin on the other hand is very professional and he keeps greeting people with the nod of his head. The staircases are narrow and there is not enough space to accommodate more than two people walking side by side. It took couple of minutes but eventually they arrive at the Gina's office. The room was full of boxes and files that placed on Gina's table. The office is smaller than her old one and the view out the window is definitely less appealing, as it is mostly facing the wall of opposite building. The other half of the window's view consists of car park. However, Gina never really cared about the perk of her previous office and seems to be oblivious of the negative changes. She takes a seat at the table while Kevin is waiting by the door.

'Ok, so you make yourself comfortable and I will see you around,' Kevin says and is about to take his leave. Gina picks up one of the boxes from the floor and starts taking the items out of it.

'You know that I am not as fragile as everybody thinks. I know I am the youngest one in the department plus a female but I am more than capable to handle what is happening now.'

Kevin stops his exit and listens quietly. Gina takes the framed pictures from the box and looks at it intensely. Eventually, she places the picture of her family on the table and continues her task of removing dirty folders from the box. 'It is extremely boring at home. I am not a big reader and I don't even have a TV. Plus, I think I am more useful here than sitting at home dwelling about what happened. And I think I deserve the ....'

Kevin knows where she is going with the last sentence and decides to end it before it gets to the point where even he wouldn't be able to resist her request of telling her more details about the case. 'Listen Kid, I do feel for you and I would love to give you more info but you know that it will not happen. I need to do my job just as much as you do and this is the dark but still vital part of the process. Your personal feelings will only damage the progress.'

Gina is getting frustrated. She has always hated to be treated as a child. Kevin raises the hands in truce before the fight begin.
'Don't get angry here Gina. You know I am right.

This is not about you being woman but you are personally involved in the case and you know where that can lead. You would say to me the same things if the roles were reversed.'

There is a slight pause as he waits for Gina to acknowledge what he said. Gina slowly nods her head and the fire diminishes from her eyes.

'Truth be told there is not a lot I can tell you anyway. This killer is erratic and extremely unpredictable.' Kevin states the fact that could be read from any newspapers that Gina can purchase from the store. Kevin turns to leave before the conversation continues any longer. He points out behind his back with the finger toward MIKEY, the IT guy. 'Ask Mikey about setting up your printer and fax machine.'

Gina, unaware tilts hear head and see the large guy sitting at the table three desks down.

Kevin closes the door behind him and Gina decides to stop the procrastination and get back to work. The sooner she starts the faster she will get more leads that would help her find the looser that likes to torture little boys.

Chapter 7

For the first time ever I feel like a real diva. I stand in front of the wardrobe contemplating my options. I cannot be easily recognised but also I can't look like some kind of hooker that would only give me unwanted attention of all the pigs on the street. I think the best choice is to take something that would cover my face as much as possible. I wear blue skinny jean, trainers with light grey vest that has a benefit of hoodie. I look at the mirror that is on the wall next to the bed and put my hair back. Perfect. This kind of style makes me look younger than 34 which only adds to my disguise. Completely satisfied, I grab the keys from the table and head out into the night.

The pub MALIBA in the corner of my street was getting fuller by minute as people usually take the time off from their busy life commitments and for some needed socialising on Fridays. The waiting time for table is over one hour so some patrons play billiard to kill extra time. However, they don't know that in couple of more hours the place would be full of drug dealers that would do anything in order to rob them of their hard-earned money. The best sellers are usually ecstasy pills and weed. I walk further into the crowd trying to be as mysterious as possible but without being considered in any way uncommon. People around here are used to weird walk-ins that are on the lookout for some anonymous entertainment. Years of being locked in and still I do recognise low-life criminals that occupied this place. I take off my hood and aim towards the very stylish bar area. Last time I was here it was just usual hole full of wooden chairs and occasional tables with one bartender. Mobsters must have started paying the owner more money in order to use the place for the dealings. Now there is a plasma TV on the wall that is used for karaoke and sport occasions, the upper part of the pub is used as a restaurant and ground floor has two small bars with more than five employees. I give young BARTENDER my most intimidating look and ask to see KENNY, the owner.

I follow her direction and walk towards the back room. The loss of manners is understandable after paying for a crime that I have not committed so without knocking I enter Kenny's office. The wall of the room is decorated by different kind of alcohols on the wooden shelves. In the middle of the room is an office table that is neat and without too much electronic equipment as Kenny doesn't consider himself to be a digital guy. If something needs to be done he has people that would do it for him, thus there is no reason for him to be learning new craft. The only thing lying on the table that is regularly used is the cheque book and account books that Kenny browse on the daily basis to ensure that nobody steals from him. The chair is facing the wall but there is nobody sitting on it. I look around suspiciously. Why would bartender send me over here if there is nobody inside?

'Karoline?' The figure slowly appears from the dark corner. I jump and scream like a little frighten girl. It must have been amusing for Kenny based on his loud laughter. He hasn't changed from the man that I used to know. He is more muscular but even before he was a quiet big guy. His dark hairs are neatly combed and he holds himself with the casual demeanour considering his chic fashion style. Why is

38

a man with such a huge power in the city wearing such a tight, short t-shirt? I asked him that once and he said that it surprises his enemies and gives his stronger leverage against them in the combat.

'You have only one more guess remaining so use it wisely,' I challenge Kenny. He is the only person that knows about me and Karoline being twins. Due to the danger of my work it was crucial to keep some of the information strictly confidential or rather completely hidden. Kenny takes a couple of seconds before he realises who stands in front of him. His eyes wide open and a huge smile covers his face. Kenny leaps towards me and an embrace that follows it takes my breath away, literally. I am not complaining though. It is nice to be finally in the company of person that likes to see me free and alive. Kenny slowly loosens up his hold of me and without taking his hands off my shoulder he looks at me.

'Oh my god girl!!! You haven't changed at all. I thought that once you are released I will no longer confuse the two of you, but it looks like you and your sister have a gift of not ageing.'

'Still a charmer I see. Shame I don't see myself with your eyes.'

'Come on Katie, don't be a party killer. Let's have a drink and celebrate your return.' Kenny takes my hand and lead me towards him most favourite spot of the room. The bar. He makes for me my number one drink, a vodka martini with twist and he takes a bottle of beer. We take a sit on the ground floor in the VIP that is not very visible. Furthermore, this table is mostly used for the business that requires not only privacy but also easy access to exit door in case something goes wrong during drug negotiation. It didn't take long and we are talking as if the last five years didn't occur. The conversation starts very ordinarily by Kenny asking about my life in the prison and how it was to be surrounded by so many tough women. We laugh about the old times and all the mischiefs that we used to get ourselves into. It is becoming clear that Kenny still trust me even after everything that has happened. There was no awkwardness between us plus the welcome I got from him doesn't give any indication that he holds grudge against me in any way. Well, the only way I can be certain about all of it is by asking.

'I spent five years in the prison, Ken.' I am sure Kenny knows where the conversation is going and he prepares for it by taking another sip of his new beer.

'I know that, Kate. And you are not the only one. Many folks working in our field spent numerous years in prison.' Kenny chinks his bottle with mine.

'But I have to say that it happened before that somebody split the organisation the way you did and managed to get away with it. Honestly, you deserve a medal for it.' Kenny laughs as he remembers the events that we were just discussing.

I don't share his humour. I certainly didn't get away with it without wounds. I paid my price and then some. 'Kenny, I need to know. Do you still believe in my innocence?'

Kenny stops laughing and rather starts concentrating on the matter at hand. He looks in my eyes while he takes my left hand gently into his. 'Of course I do believe you. Why wouldn't I? As far as I know you have never did anything to me that would prove me wrong. Sometimes people have to go to great measure in order to get what they want. I know that from experience and thus I don't see why I should be the one to judge you for your action.'

Kenny straightens up on the chair and takes out a cigar from his pocket and lights it up. 'And I am not the only one.'

'What do you mean?'

'What I mean is that there are some people who consider you to be a rat but there are many that look up to you and think of you as a hero and regardless of what happened years ago, life moves forward. There are new people on the scene, new deals and new problems that we need to deal with. Now that you are out some more issue can arise but we should be able to handle it' Kenny smiles with confidence. I look around the room and see Kenny's point. There are some people that cannot stop staring at me and whispering between each other. Never knew that I became so popular in the underworld.

I feel my face turning red due to the attention that I am receiving. Quickly, I shake it off as the memory of my sister and the reason for my visit to Kenny flashes in my memory.

'Listen Kenny, chit-chat is not why I came over here.' I make sure to lower my voice. This whole thing might be nothing. Maybe Karoline decided to play the role of herself and disappear with her mates but I need to make sure for the Suzy's sake.

'I think Karoline is missing. I went to her place yesterday thinking she will be waiting for me as it was my release day. But she wasn't there and her place is complete mess. There is also some blood on the floor and coach but no body.'

Kenny listens with interest and worry on his face which only increased my bad feeling. I didn't see or talk to my sister for years. On the contrary, Kenny became her close friend and obviously he must know when something is out of ordinary more than me.

'Ok, that is not good. But let's try to stay as positive as possible. I am sure she is ok.'

The conversation was disturbed as the crowd of mobsters enter the pub. There were not many of them, only five or six. Kenny looks behind and gives a signal to the security to keep the place in order. Security moves towards the mobsters but doesn't try to interfere if it's not necessary. Meanwhile Kenny grasps my arm strongly and pulls me back in the direction of his office. Once inside Kenny secures the door. He turns to face me and his face is no longer friendly. That doesn't scare me. I am used to Kenny's fast transformation from easy-going chap into confident businessman.

'OK, you came here for something. What is it? What do you want to know, Kate?

Ok, finally the time comes to put the cards on the table.

'I need to know who is in charge now. Why those people..?' The question is not finished as there is a loud crash coming from the main pub area. Something is not right. I slightly open the door and take a look. The mobsters that entered the place couple of minutes ago are now pushing through the crowded pub looking for somebody. I am sure that the person is me without thinking twice. The security tries to keep people calm but without success as everybody is getting anxious and ready to bolt at any moment. Couple of mobsters are heading towards the office door. I close the door and push my back against it.

'I think you need stronger security around here. Ok, so tell me who is in charge? I really need to know!' I quickly ask again.

'You will not like what you are about to hear.' There a slight hesitation in the Kenny's voice 'It is Marshall.' I am unable to fully absorb the information as I am forcefully pushed on the floor. The mobsters kick the door open and the handful of them ploughs through the door halting once they saw me.

'That is her! Get her!' one of the mobsters pointed at me while yelling the orders.

Brilliant, I can finally have some proper fun. Who knows, kicking some ass might be exactly what I need. I take my first swing and punch the leader of group with all the force, knocking him on his ass. The other men hesitate for a bit seeing what happened. That is what I hope for and before they know what hit them I am all over them. All the mobsters move back into the area of the pub trying the hardest to get themselves back under control. Kenny follows them with me and together we are showing them who is in charge here. We take advantage of everything that can be found in the room. Kenny moves next to me and get ready for some action by grapping a pool stick from the pool table. Meanwhile, men manage to get themselves back in the position and before long everybody is prepare for the upcoming fight. Two men simultaneously move towards me. One is two feet taller than me and the other one is maybe double my weight me but that doesn't scare me. I take the chair from the table and smash it on the fat guy's head. It only disturbs him for a second and then he composes himself. Meanwhile the tall guy tries to find a way to punch me a couple of times but each time I block the attack. I am surprised with how inadequate those men are. What happened with tough warriors that the underworld trained? I look back while still blocking the attack of both men and sees that there is a wall behind me. One important advice that I learnt during my martial arts and military training is to never allow to be pushed to the corner or the wall. I kick one, a fat guy in the groin. As he fells to his knees I turn around and run towards the wall but instead of stopping I jump on it and do a flip backward flying over both men. Once back on my feet I take a hold of the table in front of me and with wide swing I hit both men behind me across their faces. Meanwhile, people furiously push and run towards the door. I don't care anymore who is involved in the fight and start taking everybody down. I twist the arm of the guy in front of me, forcing him on his knees and quickly punch him with the back of my hand. Kenny starts laughing seeing how much I am enjoying myself. There is a strong punch on his back which makes him to turn back and see that two little mobsters try to take him down with two chairs which only broke in little pieces on Kenny's strong back. Kenny laughs louder and with that enthusiasm he takes both men into bear hug that is not very kind. Both men are thrashing as they are not able to breathe. Kenny increases the hug till they stop struggling and lost consciousness. My observation of Kenny's interesting approach makes me to lose truck of what is happening around me. The hit to my left check snap makes me stumble towards the pool table. Three men use my weak moment and start kicking me all around the body. I see a pool cue below the pool table and quickly reach for it. I swing the cue behind making sure that it hit all the men around me. Quickly, I get back on my feet, breaking the cue in half in order to use it more productively. The fight spreads like a wild fire all around the room. Everybody gets involved, even patrons that have nothing to with it. I use my sticks hitting people across the face and behind the knees. There is a guy on the other side of room that put his hand in the back pocket and pulls out a gun. I take the triangle from the pull and throw it straight between his eyes. The moment he would fire the gun the pub would become a graveyard as everybody would start firing at each other. Unfortunately, the smack to his face only delays him for a second and as soon as he composes himself he aims the gun straight at me with a winning grin. I tightly close my eyes, expecting the inevitable end. There is a shot and suddenly all the noise is replaced by quietness.

Chapter 8

I look all over myself expecting to see huge hole somewhere on my body. Thankfully, the confident smirk of the gun holder and shooting skills did not match and he missed his goal by couple of centimetres. Suddenly, the noise returns with vengeance and as assumed everybody start panicking.

'Freeze!!' The cops pushed through the door of the club.

'Drop the gun on the floor this instant!' another cop yells at the mobsters with guns.

I am frozen to the spot, not knowing where to go. I didn't expect to see the face of police officers so quickly after being allowed to leave the place where I encountered them on the daily basis. The mobsters could see that they are overpowered and slowly they start placing their gun on the floor. There are around ten cops standing all around the room. Most of the people are either on the floor unconscious or trying to stand up with their bleeding noses. Just as quickly as the fight started it also finishes.

Kenny walks quickly towards me and pushes me towards the exit doors trying to use all of the commotion around to our benefit without success. Just at the time that I got Kenny's silent message somebody restrains me from the back and thrust me against the wall. Subsequently, Kenny receives the same attention as me. I feel sorry that this happened. It wasn't my intention to get him into this mess but who could have known that I would be recognised so quickly. Maybe I was too presumptuous to think that five years in prison changed my appearance enough to move around the streets without anybody detecting me. Well, obviously I was wrong but maybe this little misstep can be beneficial. Kenny will be already. As he always says, bad publicity is better than no publicity. Handcuffs are placed on my hands and without delay I am led towards the police car that will take me back to the place I swore I would never return to. Once I am push into the back sit a large bold man approaches the arresting officer, Gina. DOGAN has been working with Gina since she past the police academy and this is the first time that they had any kind of dispute between each other. Gina was the one that decided to hit the club with officers. She heard that some kind of a drug deal is taking place there but had no legit confirmation from her sources. Nevertheless, she took the shot and went there without official orders. However, she didn't expect that by the time she will get to the infamous drug dealers club it would be in the swing of a fight. This is not something that her chief will appreciate very much. This kind of action can have a great damaging outcome on the undercover work of fellow detectives.

I don't know what exchange is taking place between Gina and her partner but I don't think it is anything flattering. It means that this action was not officially approved and it would be extremely difficult to corroborate this action with evidence as most of the people here have no drugs on them. The reason behind this particular bar fight was not drug-related. Furthermore, people that actually were in the possession of guns have licence to have them. Not mentioning that California law allows people to buy or win guns legally even without having appropriate permission. Good luck to the girl as he explains all this. I cannot help myself and smile a little bit. Gina girl has definitely a character and high self-confidence. I like that. This approach is needed in the profession that is dominated by men.

#

After the heated exchange both officers get inside the car. Gina and Dogan simultaneously aim for the driving seat but it is Gina who eventually take the key out and sit behind the wheel.

'Dogan, you are bleeding,' Gina says to him while passing him the napkin that she took from car storage area. Dogan touches his nose and see some blood on his fingers. He takes the napkin but doesn't offer any gratitude. Obviously, he is still annoyed with what occurred today. Dogan does have respect for Gina and like the way she thinks but he also believes in field experience and that Gina is still missing. Suddenly, there is a strong blow against the window. Dogan jumps and looks out seeing Kenny laughing at the fact that how easily he could startle the guy that arrested him.

'Son of a - - ' Dogan takes a deep breath and look at Gina.

'Listen, I will stay here and make sure that everything goes smoothly. You get out of here now.' Dogan opens the door and get out the car. 'I do hope you enjoy yourself Detective, because this is the last time that you pull this kind of shit again. At least not with me involved, I am too old to go through a disciplinary procedure and plus I don't feel like it either.' Dogan closes the door and move towards the officers that are handling other prisoners.

Chapter 9

The car moves slowly through the traffic. No words were said between us so far but I don't mind. I always welcome a little quiet. I look out of the window enjoying the scenery of San Jose. Haven't had chance yet to get acquainted with the newly built centre of the city but a brief glimpse of it from the bar gives indication that it is stunning. Maybe if I get out of it unhurt I will get a chance to go and see it. However, now I will have to stay focus and stay in the darker places in order to gain insight in what is happening in the organisation. Now that I know that Marshall is the new leader everything seems more complicated. Marshall must still feel like I betrayed him but I really hope that he didn't feel the need to punish me for it by hurting Karoline. Vengeance can force people to do things that you wouldn't expect.

'Hope you enjoyed yourself back there? I would not expect that woman like you could be a criminal if I met you on the street.' Finally, Gina decided to become social. Or maybe she suspects that I know more than I am letting her see. Of course, I wouldn't be there in the first place if I wasn't involved in something shitty.

'Well, that also means you are not very good at what you do then, officer,' I respond to her comment with the same sarcasm as I could sense in her voice. Obviously, she doesn't take me seriously due to the company that I keep but there is no reason why I should tolerate her assumptions.

'Or maybe I should call you Detective? - -What did you do to get a job in a patrol car? I thought Detective's job is more lucrative these days.'

Gina looks back at the road, clearly not believing that I have guts to speak to her so rudely. Usually, a person that is facing possible imprison is more obedient and less arrogant. She doesn't know yet that there is nothing that scares me about prison anymore.

'I don't need to explain myself to you but I rather spend my time breaking out than to be the one starting them.'

'You don't know what is fun then. We were not hurting anybody but just trying to enjoy ourselves during this boring evening. You only managed to arrest us, little girl because we got too caught up in the excitement.'

'Don't call me little girl and you should thank me. I saved your life back there by coming in that exact moment.' Gina raised her voice, slightly annoyed that I keep defying her. Certainly, I do remember that if it wasn't for this stubborn girl I would be maybe dead right now. I am not ungrateful but I will never let her know how relieved I was seeing her for the first time today. 'Do you want me to offer you a medal for doing your job? - - I don't think so.'

'I don't need a medal, just simple thanks would do it. Let me remind you again in case you were hit in the head during your excitement but have right to remain silent as everything could be used against you? Because your last statement could be considered as a confession I would suggest you stop talking now.'

I laugh and raise my hand in understanding. Ok, so she is strong-headed but not impossible to get through. Maybe now is the time to play the 'women should always help other women card'.

'Listen, I need to ask you to do me a favour.' I know this was definitely terrible beginning but girls have to start somewhere. I even add a polite smile. Call it an icing on the cake.

Gina looks at me with astonishment but says nothing. This is the first time I have a chance to look at Gina properly. She looks very young but there is wisdom in her eyes that have deep colour of forest during summer. 'The traffic today is terrible and it looks like the journey might last longer than I anticipated.'

This is not response that I was hoping for. I continue waiting with hope that her curiosity will get better of her. Gina takes the mobile and dials her partner letting him know that it will take her longer to get back to the station.

The journey continues in again in silence. I see the changes in Gina's face and know that she fights her own need to know what the favour I need is. But there is something else that is bothering this girl. She rarely smiles and the way she holds her body give indication that she is anxious and under lots of stress. If I met her before I became this empty shelf I would try to reach towards her a helping hand but now I have other things to worry about.

'I have some people that I know within the higher rank of police department. I need you to get in touch with them before we reach the station.' I try my luck one more time to get conversation started again and this time with success.

'I don't remember saying that I will do that favour for you. Plus I don't believe a word that you are saying anyway.'

'I am not lying to you. What would be my point anyway?'

'Let me guess? The contact of yours is somebody that even I would be worried to cross. Maybe even my Captain?' Gina speaks while looking occasionally back at me in the mirror. My demeanour changes from the cocky to desperate the moment Gina mention the word captain.

'Yes, I am not going to lie. The person I need to speak to is your Captain. You just need to tell him my name Kate Summers and he will confirm that he knows me. ' There is a pause as Gina response with loud laughter.

'Save it, ok. I know people like you. The only thing that a scamp from street wants is a free phone call.' Gina stops the car at the red light. Then she turns to me but keep her left hand on the wheel. 'I might consider helping you to get in touch with your lawyer. You do have rights anyway.'

I exhale disappointingly. We are almost in the station and it looks like my time is running out. Gina might be a harder cookie to crack than I thought. Without her giving me a benefit of doubts I won't be able to get in contact with Adams. I am a low-profile criminal in Gina's eyes and there is no reason for her to involve her supervisor in my case.

'What is it Kate Summers, why such a need to talk

to my boss?'

'I am looking for somebody close to me. She is missing and there is possibility that she might be dead. Your boss knows me and I believe that he might have some information about her whereabouts.' I can see by Gina's worried expression that she is in turmoil. She is a girl of honour and knowledge that there is somebody that might be in trouble and needs help seizes her attention more than silly bar disagreement.

'How long has she been gone and it would be too much to think that you have reported that to the authorities?' I am getting at this point really aggravated. It is getting really annoying that I have to justify all my actions and decisions. Why people cannot just for once give me what I am asking for. It is not like I am telling her to take the case of missing person. The only thing I need is to find out if Adams has any idea if anybody is interested in me to the point of kidnapping Karoline.

'If you want to play bad cop with me we can stop right now and you can take me to somebody who is willing to help people in need. Funny enough I thought it might be you as you are a detective that is supposed to serve and protect.' I lean back against the back seat and take a deep breath. This certainly doesn't go the way that I was expecting. I really need somebody to cut me some slack today.

'Ok, don't try anything. Let's just say I do believe you and there is somebody that you are trying to find. Tell me more about it? Who is the person and why do you think she might be in any immediate danger?'

I take the opportunity and blurt everything out from

the moment I was released till the club fight. I don't know why but I decided to keep the prison part out of the story. Don't know why though, as Gina would find out everything once she pulled out my file. But at least for a while I would like to keep a part of my life to myself. It is not fair. Usually people that were released from prison have a chance for new beginning but of course I cannot afford this luxury. Furthermore, I don't trust Gina. Not yet. But I do need her help so I need to tell her something about me that would give her an indication of what I suspect is happening. Once I am finished describing Karoline's place and Kenny's updates about new boss of the company Gina finally gave me undivided attention.

'OK, there is a case that is being handled by my department at the moment.' Gina starts explaining the progress of the case. 'I don't really think it has any connection with your sister as the information doesn't seem to match with other unsolved cases. I cannot really tell you a lot but if you have watched news you would know there is a serial killer on the loose. We have been trying to get him for some time. It is also the reason why I am - - 'Gina never finished the end of the sentence but I can guess that she was about to reveal something personal about herself. Cannot blame the girl for protecting her privacy. I would do the same if I had any. I smile with compassion letting her know that I do understand that the job that she committed herself to comes with price.

'A bit of personal time has never hurt anybody. No need to explain. But tell me more about the murders. Who knows, maybe it has something to do with the disappearance of Kristina. I cannot rule out anything at the moment.'

'So far there were six murders. The time of death is always at night but that might be due to the victims' profession as drug dealers and thieves. So far I think that is the only but still major connection between all victims.'

'Cause of death?'

Strangulation, stabbing and gun shots. Fair to say that killer doesn't get any gratification from the killing as death are too unpredictable with no unique signs that would imply work of a sadistic serial killer that likes to torture little animals.'

That makes me wonder. The killer is obviously not a sexual maniac but that doesn't make me feel any better. He is choosing people from the world that holds lots of grudge against me. If somebody found out about Karoline that would put her in lots of danger.

'So as you can see, Kate there is no reason why your sister would become his next prey. No women were attacked in the area either.' Gina is now turned completely towards me. For a second we look like two friends catching up. Of course, you would have to scratch out the part that we are sitting in the police car and instead of sitting in front I am handcuffed in the back seat.

'Do you think it is mob affiliation?' I ask hoping that Gina would to confirm my suspicion. Gina nods.

'Tell me again when the last time you saw your sis was?'

'I can tell you exactly that it was five years ago.'

Gina is surprised with the information. Of course, it is not very common for somebody to be so worried about a person that she didn't even see for number of years. Eventually, she will dig up some more into my past and then things will become clearer.

'Have you been abroad?'

'Yeah you can say that.' I nod but don't provide further details of my whereabouts. That would only made things more complicated. 'If you could please let me see my contact from within police department I would be able to sort out this mess.'

'What is the full name of Karoline?' Sometimes I feel as Gina was only hearing whatever she wants. This is the way detective works when they are trying to solve the case. They find one clue and dig deeper and deeper till something jumps out of the hole they created. But this is not an interrogation and I am no witness.

'Summers but originally it was Savinkov.' Gina keeps staring at me, evaluating every word that I say and this information gets her interest. I am sure that she was wondering where I am originally from. There is nothing on me that would make me to fit in with the Californian, glamorous population. I am not tall nor blond or trying to make it in the media business. However, if I really try I think I could succeed in the role of corrupted officer that is being persuaded by every gang lord in the LA area. My dark look and strong European features would make me a star.

'Yes, as you could gather I am not from around here. We are originally from Eastern Europe but we moved in her when we were only twelve. Eventually we decided to change the name to more traditional

American surname in order to fit in.'

'Couldn't change the accent though.' Gina slightly laughs. She doesn't know useful the accent was for me once I went undercover. People don't know that some things that were holding you back in the past could save your life in the future. However, now is the time to stop this little dialogue.

'What is this? A Spanish Inquisition into my background? I just need to talk to somebody regarding my sister and then I will be out of your way.'

'Not so fast. Why would I get you in touch with my boss regarding a missing person report? This is being handled by LAPD unit, not homicide so I would suggest you tell me exactly what is happening here. You were caught fighting very dangerous people couple of minutes ago. They were ready to pull the trigger the moment we got in and now you are telling me your sister is missing and you think it might have something to do with a case that has completely different MO. Are you in anyway involved or were involved with underworld Kate?'

I look out of the window, admiring people that have no connection with the evil that this world is hiding. I am proud of most of the decisions I have done during my career but sometimes I wish that I could be as oblivious to the danger of this city. I would love to become mother, have a loving husband and nice house that in this economy would make me work for years in order to pay off the mortgage.

I look back and Gina but I still refuse to give any more information. There is no reason to directly implement myself in something that might have nothing to do with me.

'Ok, well I am going to give you benefit of doubt and get you to my Captain. But do understand. I have no idea who you are but I can guess that you experience some awful things in your life. So let me promise to you one thing. If you are misleading me or playing some kind of game with me I will make sure that your past life will be considered walk in the park compare to hell that I will send you to.' Gina starts the engine and start moving through the traffic towards her destination. No more words are being said but her threat remained in my head. Not because I am worried or scared but because I am surprised that her warning made me feel absolutely nothing. Hell is not new to me and expectation of pain doesn't scare me. If it did I would be already dead by now.

Chapter 10

I enter the launderette and found an empty spot to sit down. I don't think Captain improved with his time management so at least I can try to get my muscles more relax. That fight did take lots of energy out of me. You would think that years in the prison would improve my stamina but maybe also age plays its role. I used to be more bendy and faster five years ago. Now I am just muscular with almost no flexibility compare to the street gang that regularly run from authority.

Suddenly, I feel a presence next to me. I don't need to turn to know that Adams is the person. Once I get a glimpse of him I am surprised how same he looks. His hands have couple of more wrinkles but otherwise it feels like I just saw him yesterday. Adams was always very lucky. Once he hit his 40s the time stopped for him and almost fifteen years later and he still looks the same.

'You know you could have just called and let me know you are free. I am always here for you so why going through all the trouble of arrest?' Adam looks at me for the first time and I am hit with the sharp emotion of respect. He was the only ally that I had while I was on the street and he not once disappointed me. It is shame that work took so much of his time that he was unable to give his generous spirit, sense of humour and commitment to special woman. He would have been brilliant husband and eventually father. Some people were born to only serve and protect and if I could choose who is going to for the rest of my life stand above watching over me it would definitely be Adams.

'I thought that you might have written it in your diary. I mean, I was one of your best so there should have been welcome party prepare for me with red carpet, cameras and fans.' I laugh hoping to release some tension. But Adams knows that prison was not a joke and I witnessed and experienced things that will remain forever in my memory.

'You were and still are a great credit to the organisation. You kept the best cover that I have ever seen but now I just don't know if it was all worth it.' Adam takes a deep breath and lightly touches my hand. I can understand his opinion. We all work hard and sacrificed a lot in order to keep the street clean but now after my release it feels like the players in the game changed but the mission remained the same. Fight still continues and I am no longer this young enthusiastic girl that believes that I can change the world for better. When I look in the mirror I see that light that used to be in my eyes every morning is now gone. I am no longer looking forward to every day but instead I am dreading it. The question is will I be able to get it back or is this end of my journey? And do I really care anymore about what will happened to me?

'Kate, you were actually so good that we were unable to replace you. The risk was just way too high.' Adams is forgetting that I know him and his way of work more than anybody else. Behaviour and work of the cognition is my passion. That is the reason why I was chosen for undercover work. It requires discipline and able to predict next step of your enemy. Currently, Adams is trying to flatter his way towards convincing me to enter the enemy's nest again.

'Please Adam stop. You don't have to tell me what a great asset I was to the organisation. I am quite aware that I was keeping the holding cells occupied at all times. However, I also know that what I have done must have got you all in lots of trouble.'

My action during that night resulted in many assholes escaping without justice being served.

'Does that mean that you don't want to return back to service? 'Adam asks me in serious tone. Adam knows that is can be beneficial for them. I already have insight and even though some people have mixed feeling about my action there is still concrete evidence that I was convicted, went to prison and never testified against anybody who is part of the crime world. Therefore, it would only take minimal effort to get me back insight the gang. Despite of the fact that I love my work I need to get my priority straight. This changed since the last time. I am no longer this free woman without worries. The memories of prison and what I went through there will ensure that I am overly conscious of my action. Underworld will smell the betrayal straight away especially if I wouldn't play by their rules. The only benefit of getting back undercover is that I might get some hints of what happened to Karoline.

'I don't know Adam. The news of my release spread fast. I am not sure what is happening but when I was in Kenny's place things were not as calm as usually. I think they are on the brink of war.'

'Maybe they were scared of you. You always knew how to awake strong emotions in people. That was always asset for us in the field. We knew that even if you were in trouble you would find your way out of it.'

'Yes, and that is why I spend so many years in prison, because I am so creative.' The flattery is starting to get on my nerves. The five years with women that suffer from narcissism made me more wary.

'Don't be too hard on yourself; you have done what was needed in order to get yourself out of the situation without raising any eyebrows about your background.'

I really think that I have to get to business now. This conversation is getting more ludicrous. How Adam dare to say that the prison sentence was the only way for me to get out of this mess. It was their case and I was only one of the puppets. Once things went downhill the people that I worked for were supposed to protect me, help me get out of it all without such a huge sacrifice. Instead I had to lose everything; my family, friends, career and reputation in order for them to cover their asses.

'Let's stop talking about the past and concentrate on what is happening now. I heard that you were bothered by a serial killer.' I can see surprise in Adam expression. He must have thought that the reason for this meeting is to discuss my future with the drug unit.

'That is not really something you should be worried about. We have it all under control.' Adam's voice returns back into business mode.

'I heard otherwise.' I stand up and start pacing in front of Adam.

'Listen, I don't want to cross my boundaries here. However, if this case is in any way mob connected than I want to be kept in the loop. I want to know everything about the cases and possible perpetrators.'

'You start to sound like it is either going to be your way or no way.' Adam smiled at me.

'Look at it whatever way you want, but these are my conditions. I help you if you help me. I am worried that my sister's disappearance has something to do with it and thus I don't want to risk her safety by ignoring potential clues. This killer is angry at mobs, I was one of them and Karoline is my sister. There might be connection.'

'Why would I help you? Just your mere presence might complicate things and destroy our investigation.' Adams also stands up and put his suit on. Still don't understand how people can wear so much clothing during this heat.

'Adam, don't try my patience. You are where you are in your investigation because of me so some gratitude would be nice. But if you really need better reason than just the fact that you owe me than here is it. You help me find my sister and I will make sure that this time you will get both the leader of the mobs and also your serial killer.'

Adams seems to be thinking but I know that I am already winner. I know him well enough to know that he will never let a deal like this to get wasted.

'Ok Kate. However, expect a rough journey. It won't be easy to get their full trust again.'

'Don't worry about me; I have my own sources.' I give Adam handshake that seals the agreement. Adam is ready to leave but I still have one more thing that I need to add. This time there will be no loose ends.

'Captain! If I decide to finish and throw the towel I want your full support and acknowledgment. Promise me that this time you will not turn your back on me'. This is the first time that I have express my disappointment at the way things were handled in the past. Adam looks at me and I see the quilt that he feels. He nods and without any further comments leaves.

Chapter 11

Kenny is at the bar ready to close it but there is still one of the DRUNK MOB members licking his wounds from the fight that occurred hours ago. Kenny approaches him, ready for confrontation.

'Listen mate, you need to leave now. I am as much beat as you are and need to sort out this mess here.'

The drunken guy looks at Kenny. He wants to raise his fist and show him who is the boss but realises soon enough that it is a lost cause. He would be defeated before he even starts fighting.

'Fine but this is the worse fucking joint that..' Kenny grasped his collar before he manages to finish the sentence and drug him to the door.

'Yea I hear ya...now fuck off.' Kenny pushes him out of the door and closes it behind him, locking the door and returning back to his office. He knows it would take him forever to sort out all the damages, plus police will be on his back 24 hours from now on so he needs to keep low profile.

The drunker start rubbing his head and slowly start moving towards his car. He uses other hand to try fishing his car key from the back pocket. Suddenly, the hair on his hand stands up. He starts looking around trying to pinpoint the reason for his feelings. There is nobody around. The drunken mop shakes his head and start laughing. He might have drunk more than he is able to handle. Time to go home and explain it to his lady. Slowly he approaches the car but before he put the key in the door he feels pain in his leg. He grasps it and angrily turns around. Maybe his imagination was not the cause of his agitation.

The shadowy figure moves from behind the tree in front of which the car is parked and approaches the drunken man. He is holding the wire in his hands. The shadow figure extends the wire and get ready to strangle the man. The job needs to be done quietly as there are still some people wondering around. Once he is two feet away from him the shadowed figure moves forwards faster and ties the wire around the drunk's neck. They are struggling for a while but it doesn't take long for the victim to fall on the floor. But he is not dead, only a little bit paralysed. He decides to use different, more messy approach. He takes out the knife from his pocket and start stabbing the coughing guy in the chest. It takes more than ten stabs to get the man to stop moving but just to ensure he is dead the killer stabs him one last time in the heart and quickly disappears back into darkness.

\#

The sun is shining outside. People walking on the street minding their own business. It always makes me wonder what other people think about while they go through the day. Are their worries in life similar to mine? I learnt long ago that people are all different which makes them equally unique. Some people consider financial assets and career to be the crucial element in their life. Other concentrate more on spending time with family and money are only secondary. I need to wonder while I am drinking my coffee at Rose Coffee shop just across from my flat what drives people forward. What excite them? What scares them? My thoughts return back to present when Gina rushed through the door. Obviously the girl is worried that my meeting with Adams didn't go well which would result in her being fired. Gina sits down across from me and I cannot help but make her sweat a bit more.

'We are on.' I know that this admission is way too brief but there is not lot to say. I am back in but this time I am doing it for a reason bigger than career advancement.

'Did you have a choice or they force you to get back in?' Gina's curiosity can be adorable. One day she will learn that chit-chat between undercover officers will not reveal a lot of information. Usually the meetings are short and brief.

'In this case I had many choices. I need you to get me the entire file relating to the case. I don't care how relevant or irrelevant you think they are. I want it all. Bring it all to this address.' I pass her my address written on the little piece of paper. I finish my black Americano and throw five dollars on the table. It is time to go home and finally get some rest. Between the meetings and fights I didn't have a chance to get any sleep or nutrition. I won't be good for anybody in this condition.

'Wait, you are already leaving? I thought we will discuss what happened with the captain.'

'There is nothing that needs to be discussed. I told you we are on.' I know I might be bit harsh with her but there is no time for pleasantries. I need to do my job in order to find out where is my mother of my niece. I take my keys from table and leave without giving Gina second thought. She knows what needs to be done.

Chapter 12

Slowly I entered the Karoline's flat hoping that this time I will find no surprises. Luckily, the flat has remained the same messy way as I left it.

'My god I am tired but I cannot continue living like this.' I think some spring cleaning is necessary. Firstly though, I need to put something in my stomach. Wouldn't it be funny that day after release I fainted due to the starvation? I went to the kitchen hoping that Karoline was more responsible now when she was mother. OK where can I possibly find something suitable to consume. I open the fridge that is covered with numbers of different magnets and child paintings. Looks like Suzy is growing to be a little artist. One of the pictures gets my attention. There are three people on it. One is the small one which I assume must be Suzy. The second one is taller with dark hair and green eyes and the third one look similar but slightly smaller. It looks like me and Karoline. Not knowing how, I started to cry. I cannot believe that after so many years Suzy still remembers me. She was a tiny child when I was taken away.

'BANG BANG!!!!' I quickly turn ready for a fight but there is nobody there. Looks like somebody forgot how to knock on the door without waking the whole bloody building. Close to the main door I see the envelope on the floor. I pick it up and look at it closely. There is no indication what can be inside.

'Who are you really Kate?' Gina's voice echo in the corridor.

Now I have an idea what this is all about. Gina must find out who I really am. Inside the envelope are papers all concerned with my mob affiliation and assumed betrayal. I don't need nor feel like reminding myself what happened and I certainly don't feel like I own somebody any explanation. It is funny how people tend to assume that they know the true when the only things they have are point of views of different people. The people which might not even been part of the event in the first place.

'What you don't understand? The file clearly states who I am or rather who I was. I used to be a cop and due to unfortunate circumstances I am no longer one.' Again I am getting back in time thinking what would happened if I refused the undercover job offered to me by Adams. The longing of different life bring me sorrow so I shake it off. Humans are creature of repetition. Everybody always say that trial and time in prison is punishment for any wrong doings. However, the true is the quilt will never disappear. Every day for the rest of my life I will think about my action and therefore the punishment will never end. Prison was just one stop during this bus road to atonement.

'Will you let me in? I am starting to get looks. It is not considered healthy to be speaking with the door you know.'

Slightly I smile and open the door. Don't know why but I like to make her irritated. No reason why she should believe that life in the force is easy. I take the jacket and get out of the flat locking it.

'Where are you going? We need to discuss our plan!' Gina backs off but still doesn't allow me to pass.

'We?' How this girl make a conclusion such as this? I only met her day ago and she thinks we are partners. Well time to bring her out of the dream.

'Firstly, I didn't ask you to bring me a file of my past. I wanted information about the mobs and serial killers.' I look around just to make sure nobody is eavesdropping. This building is full of old people whose entertainment is to keep up with latest gossip.

'Well while I getting information about your mobs surprisingly I found out that you are one of them. Little titbits you forgot to mention it.'

'You know everything that is needed. You should keep at your line of work as you wouldn't be a good researcher. I was not a mob member but I was undercover. I don't have time to be explaining to you my life. I guess this file you gave me is only one part I asked you for. Do you have information about the mob hater killer?'

Gina still doesn't trust me but I know there is not a lot she can do. Now I have Adams's support. Gina passes me file.

'Is everything in here?

'Yes of course there is.'

'Good! Now go home and I will keep you in the loop.' I turn to leave but hand on my arm stops me.

'What do you mean go home? This is my case

and..'

'Nooo, this is not your case. You were taken off it so actually you are going against your orders.'

I shake her hand off me swiftly and again try to get away but Gina is determined to make it as difficult as possible.

'You are forgetting, Kate that without me you have nothing. Yes, Captain is on your side but I was told to be your inside person. So yes, it is my case and whether you like it or not I am your partner.'

'As I said I will keep you in the loop. I need to go visit a friend and believe me if I bring you around the whole thing will go to hell. Give me time to figure the connection.'

Gina finally let me go. She knows that it would be dangerous for all of us if somebody find out that Gina is a cop.

'Fine, but I want to be there once things start getting shape.'

'And you shall be.'

Chapter 14

Back in the coffee shop I spread around all the information that Gina gave me. I look at the pictures hoping that something will jump out of me as unusual but it seems like the only thing that they have in common were the association with mobsters and drug dealers.

'Excuse me Madam. Would you like something to eat or drink?'

My god, do I look old or something. Why do people talk to me as if I was in my fifties.

'Coffee and chicken sandwich will do.'

The waitress doesn't move so I look up to see what the problem is. One of the pictures was face up and it seems to interest the young woman. I turn the picture back face down.

'That is all and don't call me Madam again.'

'I am sorry!' The girl move away, quickly worried that I might possibly let her boss know about her little voyeurism.

I take the pile of pictures and report from the medical examiner. The cause of the death is almost always same; either strangulation, stabbing or cut throat. The killer is obviously looking for specific victims within the mob world which means that he might have some kind of history with them. I assume that the killer is a male as some of the victims are too big to be overpowered by woman. I feel like killings are drive by personal agenda. Furthermore, the killer was able to get information about those victims before he killed them. That means that he is educated and has purpose in mind. Once I find out what that purpose is I will know who is behind it. I look at the pictures of the victims and see no link between them. They work for the same bosses but it doesn't look like they have any professional or personal connection. One picture stands up from all the others. It is young boy. He is bold, 5'7 feet tall and very slim due to drug dealing. His features indicates that he got into this line of work because of his own addiction. However, his youthful face and deep green eyes makes me feel like I know him.

The TV got louder. I look at the screen to see what all the commotion is. The news reporter stands in front of yellow tape and talks to the camera. The waitress came over and places my order on the table.

NEWSREADER: *"It is well-known knowledge that police department believe that these killings have connection with the mob conflicts. So far all the victims have been in some way associated with the underworld crime syndicate that is currently running wild throughout our city."*

I try to look behind the reporter hoping to see what is happening behind him. However, it is impossible to see anything besides officers walking around the crime scenes and collecting evidence.

'Well, it looks like I will have to call Gina earlier than I thought.'

NEWSREADER: *"There are still questions about the light approach that police has taken to deal with this cases. However, the main question that remains same is if this is the work of single individual that is looking for justice or revenge or is group of different mobs fighting against each other?"*

In the background I can see Gina working on the crime scene. That reminded me of first time I met her. The first thing that got my attention were her eyes. Such a deep green I have not seen ever in my life …till today. I look back at one of the picture and see the similarity between one victim and Gina. I take my laptop and type Selby name into the search. Thousands of links came up. I reduced the findings by country and city. One of the article had titled that will possibly confirm my suspicion "Second victim of the mob killer is connected with law enforcement". The victim was found four months ago; he fits the bill of all the others victims that were low-level gagsters. The name of the victim is HARRY SELBY, a 22-year-old man.

It seems like I was not the only one keeping secrets. Finally, I understand Gina's eagerness to find the killer. She is after the same thing as I am: 'revenge'.

Chapter 15

Gina walks inside the bar with another inspector trying to relax after her confrontation with incompetent ROOKIE. She cannot believe that somebody would be so stupid to actually send an untrained officer in the middle of the crime scene. This is not a training field for people to learn how to do their job. That idiot has almost destroyed important evidence.

'Low-level mob figure that moves in the wrong circle. He was killed in the brutal manner. Definitely our guy.' Gina concluded while she moves around the Kenny's bar trying to see if there is view on the crime scene from the window. If there is then, maybe somebody has seen something.

'I know what you are thinking, Selby but nobody has seen anything. He was the last one here and after the door closed the owner and the only person left in here moved back into his office,' Dogan states while he moves to stand next to her. 'Are you sure that his is our guy? I mean previously his MO was slightly different. This time he chose open space and the manner of killing is disorganised. Doesn't fit the previous profile.'

Gina cannot believe her ears and abruptly turns towards him looking as she is just about to attack him.

'Are you kidding me?'

'NO listen. This guy was stabbed numerous times. It almost looks like he wanted to gut him alive. I believe that this is just opportunistic killing. There was a disturbance here just couple of days ago and there is a big chance that the low life outside pissed somebody off enough to do this to him'.

'NO! It couldn't have been opportunistic. There is no sign of robbery and neither fighting. If they have really known each other from a previous encounter than there would be some kind of indication in the crime scene. But there is absolutely nothing there. It means that it was premeditated.' Gina is not willing to let go.

'I am not going to continue this conversation and waste our sources on this hellhole. He was at the wrong time at the wrong place and that is it. We have a serial killer to catch and I need as many people looking for him as possible.'

Gina looks at Dogan with resentment. She thought that he had her back but it looks like he is just another cop trying to get his name of the wall of fame without going extra mile. The mob killer case is now the top priority and everybody is trying to prove to the big bosses that they are able to solve it. However, there is only one thing that could be worse than not finding the killer and that is to arrest the wrong one.

'But don't worry, we picked up everything from the scene and if there is any connection between this death and other killings than we will deal with it.'

'Sure you will. I am surprised with you Dogan. Are you so scared that you might be wrong that you are letting fear to cloud your judgment?'

Dogan only gives Gina disapproving look without any response.

'OK everybody lets wrap it up here!' Dogan yells and walked out of the bar.

Gina is still standing against wall cannot believe her eyes.

Chapter 16

Twenty minutes later I found myself walking down the dark street. The day passed by very quickly and the sun disappeared behind the horizon. I remember the sun I saw the day I was released. I promised myself that I will enjoy every warm touch of sunlight. Unfortunately, again I was forced into shallow darkness that seemed to have no ending. I keep wondering if I have done something so terrible in my past life and this is some kind of retribution that I am not aware of. The mobile start buzzing in my back pocket but I just couldn't be bothered. I know where I am going and maybe this time I will get my answers. I haven't been in this area for five years but nothing changed. The streets are full of the homeless people and drug addicts looking for their next fix. In the corner I see the person that haven't change at all, IVAN. Still too tall, too skinny and way too arrogant for his own good. Ivan is just about to get his next fix as I approach him and kick it out of his hand.

'Hallo Ivan. I hoped that years in this jungle made you change your way. I see I was wrong.'

Quicker than the panther he gets up and run towards the alley. Great, I needed some exercise. I pursue him without too much effort. The years of only exercising and making sure that everyone stays out of my way got me ready for almost anything. I am forced though to knock some people on the floor as they always seem to find a way to stand exactly where I need to be. Ivan changed his approach and ran inside the butcher shop. He ignores people around him and sprints towards the back door. I am still not far behind him but instead of running past the people I leap through the counter and push the cashier away from my path. Ivan opens the back door and is almost run over by the trash truck. He backs up and wait for the car to pass before he continues with his silly attempt to escape. I emerge from the different door and sprint down the alley using the advantage of the empty area. Not far away from me is Ivan still thinking I will get out of the same exit door. He was never very bright but at least he love good gossips. Today might be his lucky day. I stop running and instead start walking towards him hiding behind the wall of the residential building.

'Can we try again Ivan?' I knock on his right shoulder with the smile. 'This is not the welcome I was expecting.'

Ivan looks at me with fear. That is quite surprising as I have never hurt this little shit. Instead I kept him out of the prison where he should have rotted anyway for distributing the drugs around the street. He tried to move but this time I grab him around his neck and throw him against the wall. How does he dare to treat me as an enemy after everything I did for him?

'How did you manage to get out?'

'Oh, you mean when I got out.' Just for the sake of it I make my grip on his neck a bit more uncomfortable. 'Hope you missed me?'

Ivan struggle against my hand but without success. I was and still am more powerful than he could ever be. And this time it is not just about my connections but also about his fragile body strength.

'I need information and you are going to provide me with them. Let's just call it a repayment of sort.' I kick his lower legs from the back and get him on his knees and take the gun out. All the fun comes to the end one day.

'Listen little man, I don't have time for this crap. I am looking for a missing woman related to me and a serial killer. Tell me what you know.'

'I know nothing. I am just a drug distributor.'

Ok, so I already committed some horrendous things in the past. One more murder shall not weight heavily on my conscious.

'Ok well have it your way.' I aim the gun towards his head. No reason to make it more painful for him.

'Wait!! I don't know anything about missing woman or serial killer. But honestly you are barking up the wrong tree here. Long time ago I lost track with what is happening in the big places. After your arrest people became more careful. Maybe you should visit Ralph?'

Seeing the true in his eyes I release him and put my gun back in the behind the belt.

'Ralf MacDel?'

Ivan nods. Why should I visit somebody that used to be regular customer of Marshall during the time he was only a drug dealer?

'Ralf is nobody. How can he be any use to me?'

'Ralf became the owner of the AMARETO club.' Ivan tries to get his breathing under control. Maybe I was rougher with him than I though.

I wave Ivan off. He didn't give me information that I needed but he provided me with the name of new member of the clan. Amareto club was always used for drug dealing and Ralf becoming an owner can only means that now he is part of the powerful group of criminals. I believe congratulations are in order.

Chapter 17

My head is still buzzing with the information that I received from Ivan when I get back to Karoline's flat. By the door Gina is waiting for me.

'Have you been here the whole time?' I stop before I proceed to the door. This is getting slightly ridiculous.

'Of course not. I went to office and came here five minutes ago. I though you are ignoring me again so I waited before I knocked again.'

I released the breath I didn't know I was holding and move towards the door. Gina stands too close to me and sees that I actually don't have the key from the door.

'Before you ask. The lock is loose and I didn't have time to talk to landlord yet to replace it.'

Gina doesn't question me but instead passes me bottle of red wine that she took from the shopping bag and get inside.

'You came here to get wasted?' The Shiraz. My god, I used to love nice glass of red years ago but things changed. Now I prefer a proper drink. Got only one life and everything should be done with the 'bang'.

'No, I came here to give you some information that

might interest.'

Closing the door behind me I proceed towards the kitchen and got wine glass from the cupboard. In the bar I found nice bottle of Russian vodka and pour myself nice glass with ice and lime. Slowly, I get back to the living room and see Gina admiring some of the pictures that are on the wall. I sit on the couch and put the glasses down.

'You have many pictures with this child. Who is she?' Gina shows me the picture that she is holding. Suzy is there playing with cat and opening Christmas presents.

'It is my niece Suzy. My sister's daughter.'

'Tell me about your sister,' Gina askes as she sits down next to me. I keep looking at her trying to figure out what is her motive. Why this little girl care about my life so much. As hard as I look I can see no deceit. It might be good for me to talk with somebody. I have to admit that I miss my regular visit to Caroline. I was thinking to use the card she gave me and give her a call. But maybe this will do it too.

'My sister was always the perfect child in the eyes of my parents and others. She must have some kind of talent that get people believing that she is an angel that means no harm. Even after she got knock up while she was sixteen she still remained a saint to everybody around her.' I couldn't keep the smile out of my face. Any memory of my sister makes me happy. Plus who would look at her little niece and says that she was mistake. She is a perfect child and joy to the family.

'You must know how difficult it is to keep younger

siblings out of trouble?' I look at Gina and as expected the surprise in her face is more than visible.

'I should have known that you would put two and two together. I mean you used to be cop.' Gina relaxes but I still can see that she didn't want to get into this subject.

'Harry was very good kid but from the young age we were exposed to the worst in the world. We lived in the rough neighbourhood, rough school and rough parents. Eventually we both ended up on the different side of the law. Don't take me wrong. Harry would never hurt anybody. Not even an animal but he did want to fit in. He wanted to be accepted somewhere in this world and unfortunately he did not choose the best crowd. I did try to help him...' Suddenly Gina stopped talking. I can see that it makes her very upset.

'It must have been very hard for you.'

'You wouldn't believe how many times we had a talk and how many time I turned a blind eye on his action. I was so worried that one of the people that he was working for would find out who I am and use him to get to me.'

This admission gets close to my heart. This is something that I was equally worried about in the past. I always worried that due to my ambitions Karoline and Suzy might get hurt. I place my hand on her shoulder and give it as squeeze of support. For a while we sit in the awkward silence.

'You said that you have some information for me?' I take my glass from the table and take a sip. The safest thing now is to return back to the subject that doesn't make either one of us uneasy. Gina looks at me thankfully. She is grateful to get back to business even though she came here hoping to build the friendship. Neither one of us is yet ready to give somebody that much trust. She takes a piece of paper from her jeans back pocket and passes it to me.

'What is that?'

'This is the lead that might help us to find more about the serial killer case and hopefully about your sister's disappearance. My informer told me the guy on this picture is somehow connected with the killer. Apparently all the killings happened close to either his residence or his work.' I keep looking at Gina as if she grew a second head.

'Is the guy a mobster?'

'Yes, of course.'

'Gina I think you should fire your informer. This lead means nothing. If he is mob than it is more than expected that he will be in the close proximity of the crimes.' Slowly I open the picture and as I thought it is somebody that I would never suspect.

'This man on this picture is like family to me and now you telling me that he is in some way implicated in the murders?'

'Listen, this is the lead that I got from my informer and I made a decision to show it to you in case it is in some way relevant but I have no idea in what way if any he is connected to this case. But don't you think we should check it anyway?'

The more I think about it more I want to listen to my inner voice that starts to trust this little girl in front of me. Maybe my association with the underworld is blinding me to the truth.

'Ok let's do it your way and check it out.' I move away from the couch and take my jacket. I can feel that Gina is not following me so I turn to see what is holding her.

'Now? I thought that we...' Gina points at the unfinished bottle of wine.

'You thought wrong.'

Chapter 18

The drive towards our destination was extremely quiet even for my liking. After thirty minutes I stop the car stop before Kenny's house.

'You stay here and make sure that nobody sees you.'

Silently I close the car door and move to the double floor house in the middle of nowhere. Kenny always liked privacy and what is better place than Ciudad de San Jose. The place in a remote location but still close enough to the centre of the action. The light is off but a flicker of the curtains make me believe that there is somebody in. Lightly I knock on the door. Soon enough the door are sharply opened revealing sexy blond, early 20s, short but with a big attitude judging by her annoyed expression. The girl must be Kenny's current conquest. I do have to congratulate to Kenny for his choices. The girl now only wearing shorts and large man t-shirt could pass for the model.

'What do you want?'

'I want to speak to Kenny.' I calmly answer not quite comprehending her resentment towards me.

'Yeah, sure you do.' The girl tries to close the door in my face but my foot doesn't permit it. Without invitation I force myself in determine more than ever to find out what is happening her. I am sure that in my short time out I didn't have a chance to get another enemy but this girl looks like I killed her favourite toy.

'Hey who the hell do you think you are? You cannot just burst onto someone else's property!'

I take my gun out ready to get the girl shaking when Kenny makes an entry with a red apron and towel in the hand. Looks like I disturbed some domestic action. Still, it is hilarious to see a man of his power being in such a feminine situation. Looks like I am not the only person that changed because of love.

'At ease, LEAH.' Kenny takes Leah's hand and pull her away from me. Still looking at me Kenny tries to calm the situation with his lady.

'She is my friend and you know it so there is no reason for this bickering. I thought we already went through the jealous time in our relationship.' Kenny laughs as he pushes Leah behind his back, looking slightly uncomfortable.

'Now what brings you here? Don't tell me that people don't feed you at home and you had to come all the way here to get slice of bread?'

I keep my expression strong knowing that it is killing Kenny that he cannot read my thoughts but this is just too good to pass on. A huge man like him should have ego as mountain but instead he is this romantic man that is at home cooking for his woman. If I had a camera with me I will post it on my Facebook or Twitter, whatever it is that children used this day.

'I came here to see how are you holding up after what happened today?'

'You mean after the greatest fight that my club had a privilege to be part of? Shit girl, you know how great it is to have you back. I felt like there was no excitement in my life anymore.'

Kenny stops talking as Leah gives him a little punch on the shoulder. I smirk knowing that he just got himself into more trouble than before.

'I meant excitement at the workplace, I have a lot of it in my personal life.' Saving the situation for a while Leah moves towards the living room table and sit down taking the cigarettes. Her eyes, though remain on me and every move I make.

'Kenny can we speak more privately.' I keep staring at this girl, annoyed. Her face annoys me now and I don't feel like revealing anything while she is present.

'No,' Leah jumps in again.

'Just ask whatever. You can trust Leah. She just has a little jealous temper that is all.' Kenny invites me to sit at the couch.

'I came to see if you know anything about the killings that are happening around here recently?' Kenny sits at the table close to Leah and takes a drag of her cigarette. For a while there is quiet but eventually Kenny nonchalantly shakes his head.

'No of course. But honestly I think the whole thing about serial killer is over exaggerated. You know people always keep dying in our line of work and it is not something that we should try to resolve. People in the underworld had many skeletons in the wardrobe and lots of time they need to pay for them at some point. As you know.'

Kate is not sure about it. She takes a look around trying to see something out of ordinary but she knows that she cannot look suspicious to Kenny so she moves towards the table in the corner and pick up the framed picture of Kenny and Leah. Her eyes however move around the table trying to see any kind of documents that might help her to find out what is happening.'

Not sure if I should believe him I look around trying to find some kind of clue that Kenny is not being honest. Instead I found the wall full of framed pictures of Leah and Kenny.

'Wow, you already collect pictures together. Sweet!' Leah again jumps like a little cat but this time I am ready.

'Just chill woman, I have not come here to steal your man. I have enough of them where I come from.'

Kenny starts laughing, knowing that I am telling the truth. During my time in underworld I never had problem to find somebody that would willingly warm my bed. However, there was only one person that I wanted to keep in my bed permanently, Marshall.

'Kenny, I strongly believe that killings which are happening can in some way be connected to Karoline's disappearance.'

'I don't think so Kate. I mean Karoline was very

distraught after you were taken to prison but I did keep eye on her as I promised to you. She was doing really well so there is no reason to suspect any foul play. Maybe she just went back to her old ways.'

Obviously, Leah has enough of my presence and storms out of the living room and into the kitchen.

'I don't think so Kenny. She would never start taking drugs again. Not after she almost lost Suzy during the delivery.'

Karoline still blames herself for not being more careful during her pregnancy. She was always too high and didn't realise that she missed her periods three months in the row. Once the doctor confirmed that she was pregnant everything changed, but still the pregnancy was risky due to her drug use. Suzy was on the machine and it was a miracle that she managed to survive without any permanent damage.

'Kate I don't know what to say. I really want to help but I don't know how. We used to talk almost every day but couple of days ago she stopped returning my calls. Then you came back to the picture and she disappeared. That is what I know.'

I look at him and see that he is as desperate as I am. Whatever Gina's informer said cannot be true. I don't see why Kenny would hurt Karoline. After my arrest they became as good friends as I used to be with Kenny and I trusted him with my own life.

'Would it bloody kill you to bring me some proper booze. You do own a fucking bar for God sake!!!'

Leah screams from the kitchen.

'Okay, I think this is my cue to leave. I can see you have your hands full with this one.'

I approach him and give him a quick hug.

'Don't I know it. Are you sure you don't want to stay for some burnt pizza?'

'As appealing as that sounds I don't think that it is such a good idea. Have a good evening Kenny.'

I head back towards Gina's car but something stops me. I turn back to see if maybe Kenny is behind me but see nobody. I shake it off but still move faster to my destination.

Gina is leaning against the car and curiously watches me approaching.

'He is not your guy just as I told you and I think somebody is trying to feed you with this bull shit to delay the investigation. No, let's go I feel like something is about to happened.'

Not giving Gina change to respond I open the door.

'Now wait a minute? I am...'

'Gina, please get inside the car and we will talk about it later.'

Annoyed, I get out of the car ready to drag this little girl by the neck but instead I concentrate on the shadow near the bushes. It seems as somebody is trying to get into Kenny's place and this has nothing to do with them. Quickly, I bolt in the shadow's direction. By the time I got there the person is gone. I look around but only thing I can hear is quiet. Terrible quiet; not even birds are around. Suddenly, there is a noise of broken wood and I start running again. I see the figure running towards the nearby wooden park so I speed up. It's hard to see through the thick trees that are blocking out a lot of the ambient city street light. I lost him again.

'Shit!'

I stop again but see nothing. However, I still feel the presence of somebody. He must be here somewhere. I look around and the only place he can be hiding at is the bushes across from me. I move there but surprisingly the figure jumps out and knocks me to the ground. I drag him down with me and punch him to the jaw hoping that it would weaken him. On the contrary, it looks like I only made him angrier. I take his hands and try to move them behind his back without success. Whoever this is, he is strong. Not knowing how, he uses his legs to get me in the grip and turns me around. Now I am disadvantaged and he uses it as much as possible. His hands with great accuracy punch me numerous times in the stomach and face. I manage to use some effective blocks and only get couple of hit but I have no space to return the attack. The attacker takes the knife out ready to finish me off but miraculously there is a jogger coming our way. I don't know who would run in this place during this hour but I am extremely grateful that somebody like that exists. The attacker put his knife back into the pocket, hits me one last time in the face before he retreats.

Chapter 19

Not sure where I am but suddenly I feel very peaceful. I must be dreaming or maybe the punch to the face got me unconscious. I am lying in the bed, beneath the covers and feel something that I never thought I would feel again. I am happy. One of my leg is sticking out of the cover, revealing the tattoo of the Greek Goddess of Justice, Astrea that is on the edge of my lower leg. This tattoo represents everything that I used to believe in. Justice, power and honesty. A figure emerges from the bathroom but I cannot see who it is. He has towel only around his waist but his body faces the drawer. Looks like he is looking for something. Whoever this person is he is the source of my happiness. Eventually the man turns and I see the face of somebody that I dreamt to spend the rest of my life with.

Suddenly I am forced out of the dream as the jogger splashes a little bit water on my face. Slowly I sit up and look around me.

'Don't worry, the police and ambulance are on the way.'

I get up despite the jogger's protest and start walking away.

'Thank you for being here.' That is all that I needed to say. The last thing that I need now is to get police on my case. I need to stay low now.

Back in the flat I jump to the shower. Need to get blood and dirt out of me. The mysterious figure didn't hurt me as much as he wanted but still need to rest a bit. The shampoo together with the dirt and blood slowly trailing down my legs. Even my tattoo is barely visible through all of it. I stop my movement as I hear a bang from the living room. What is happening today? Is it some kind of Attack on Kate holiday or something? Quietly I turn off the water and grabs a towel. As I peak from barely closed bathroom door I see a person on the knees picking up something from the floor. It is visibly a woman. I take a handle of the broom and move behind the woman ready to ask questions as she suddenly turns and screams like a little fox.

'What do you think you are doing?!!'

Standing in front of her is DALENA. Lady in her 50s, same height as mine, same hair, same colour but completely different personality and view on life. She is holding broken picture in her right hand and almost empty bottle of vodka in her left hand. The broken glass tripped the old woman as she tries to move away from me.

'Bloody stupid woman! Dalena what the hell are you doing here and how did you get in in the first place?'

Dalena still clutches the bottle of vodka and picture while she tries to get to her feet. Her make-up is all around her face giving indication that she must have been out drinking for hours now.

'Don't call me Dalena.'

'Why? It is the name on your birth certificate.' I start walking back to the bathroom to get the robe.

'If I am not mistaken your certificate states that I am your mother so treat me as one!'

Wearing my bathrobe I return back to living room. Dalena is now sitting at the kitchen table obviously waiting for me. I take a glass, making myself a coffee and check if all the knives are at their place. Don't want to find one in my back coincidently. That woman never liked me. Taking a deep breath I turn, ready for anything.

'Ok. What do you want?'

'I am looking for my daughter, Karoline. She always calls me. What did you do to her?' Dalena looks at me accusingly but I don't give her satisfaction of fear.

'What the hell are you implying here? What do you think I could have possibly done to your precious daughter?'

'I don't know, you are the convicted criminal in here not me!' The screaming continues but I know that in the state that this woman is in she will not be able to win even if she would want to and honestly she doesn't even have the energy to be dealing with this bullshit. As I am ready to take my leave I realises that there is something amiss. Or someone.

'Where is Suzy?'

'Oh, now you are asking. You don't worry my

lovely granddaughter is safe and taken care of.' Dalena places the broken picture on the table and aim for the fridge looking for any booze. Not caring that we share blood I take her neck and push her back towards the fridge door ready to end her miserable life.

'Listen to me old woman. This isn't a game and I am not your puppet. Tell me where my niece is now or I will beat it out of you if I have to.' I lean closer to her to ensure that she understand even in her condition that I am deadly serious with my threat.

'Suzy is ok. She is with my new boyfriend Roger at my place.' The pressure against her neck increases as I get angrier by second.

'What the hell you doing. Let me go I have told you where is she?'

I abruptly release her but still keep myself in her personal space as she fall to her knees holding her neck.

'You left my niece with a stranger that you have probably just met? Are you insane?!'

'He is a good guy and he loves Suzy so don't panic, ok. Plus you are not perfect yourself so don't you dare lecturing me about my – '

'I have paid a big price for my mistake however you on the other hand are still wondering around this country without any punishment your negligence so shut your mouth and leave me the hell alone!'

I take her jacket that she still wears and drag her towards the door. Cannot have her in my presence for another second without doing something that I might regret in the future.

'I think after so many years you should know that we get along the best when we don't see or speak to each other.'

I throw Dalena out not-so-gently.

'But I am warning you, old woman. Once I deal with my business here I will come for Suzy and if something happened to hear meanwhile I will make you and your Roger pay. Keep that in mind.' As I am about to close the door Dalena delivers one more blow.

'You were and you still are the most useless person I know and the only thing you have in common with my lovely Karoline is the pretty face of yours. If you weren't twins I would think that you were given to me by mistake.'

'That is wishful thinking on your AND my end too.' I slam the door in Dalena's face. As I lean against the door I wonder why I feel no regret or pain from the words the woman said to me. Who knows, maybe I created inside of me some kind of antinode against her. Enough procrastination, time to get back to work. I am sure the person who attacked me is the man I am looking for.

Chapter 20

Early in the morning Gina got to the station thinking about the recent development. Especially about the fact that there is somebody in the department that is either trying to mislead her by giving her incorrect information or they are hiding something much more sinister. There can be many different reasons why somebody would try to get Kenny behind bars but it just doesn't make sense why to sacrifice one person to cover up someone else crimes if there are bigger fish on the street who would fit the profile more accurately than Kenny. The only reason that comes to Gina's mind is that somebody knows that Kenny is connected to Kate. Maybe this whole tings is some kind of punishment for Kate's betrayal. It would fit the profile. The killing started shortly before Kate release, her sister's disappearance and Kenny's implication in all of this. She still believes that Kenny is somehow involved in all this. There is no indication that the person killing is not part of their group. Maybe Kenny feels need to get revenge on everybody who was responsible for Kate's conviction. The motive is there but some many puzzles are missing. Why would Kenny start killing now so many years after the event on the roof? What Karoline has to do with all this? Finally at her desk Gina keep mentally going through all the evidence that they have on the case.

Kevin steps inside the office but Gina doesn't acknowledge him. He places a folder on her table

'Bloody hell man, can you sometimes give me

some sign that you are around?!' Gina says angrily.

'Sorry Selby, but I just couldn't resist. You look like you are in clouds somewhere for a while so wanted to help you back to earth.' Kevin smiles politely while he sits in the guest chair.

'What are you working on so early in the morning?' Kevin enquires, ready to hear more. Seems like everybody is lately running around busy while he has nothing to do. The mob case got cold as the whole unit deals with the mob killer.

'I will tell you when you get me coffee. I am tired and cannot concentrate without caffeine in my brain.'

'Cool, on it now.' Kevin moves quickly towards cafeteria just across from Gina's office to get Gina her precious little energy drink. Five minutes and he is back ready to do his little questioning.

'Here you are, brand new.' Kevin passes Gina her coffee.

'I was wondering. Have you seen my file that was on my office table and suddenly disappeared?'

'Say again sir?' Gina asks pretending as she heard the news for the first time.

'The paperwork doesn't just disappear. The only explanation is that I might have left it in the printer but still thought that I would check with you as it seems like you are the only one on the 'tight schedule' recently. Which brings me to the idea that you must have some clues. And as mob killer case is classified and not accessible to you it makes me wonder how is it possible that you are the only one that seems to be the most busy?' Kevin observes Gina for any indication that she knows what he is talking about but without success.

'Understand Gina. I don't want you to be running the street trying to confront and also warn potential suspects. That would be very unreasonable.'

Gina smiles with understanding but reveal nothing. Kate needed the file and Adams gave her green light to provide her with anything without questions.

'I understand and I do assure you that I did not see or take you file from your office.'

'Ok, you go back to work and we talk later about your recent whereabouts,' Kevin smiles and after what seems like forever leaves the office.

Gina lean on the chair as Kevin closes the door and keeps looking at it for couple of seconds. That was very close call.

Chapter 21

As the evening approaches and rain finds its way to the ground Kevin walks out of his building. He is desperate to talk to his INFORMER and find what is happening behind his back. The secrecy and curious looks that Gina keeps giving to everybody around makes him nervous. Something is happening and he needs to get more information so he can get ready for whatever is coming. It looks like the weather is also not on his side today. In the distance there is a small coffee place where Kevin sees a dark figure jumping slightly from one foot to another. It seems like his young informer doesn't grasp the idea of waiting inside where is warm and dry.

'Didn't I tell you to wait for me inside? It doesn't look at all suspicious that you are waiting in the rain while there is perfectly dry place just behind you.' Kevin points to the coffee shop behind him that seems to be now completely packed with people trying to hide from the miserable weather.

'Sorry man, didn't want to miss you so I decided to wait here where I can see people. Inside it is completely full and I couldn't see anything from my table.' His Informer apologises with the childish demeanour. Plus he still continues jumping around which annoys Kevin immensely.

'What the hell is wrong with you? Stop jumping around and let's go inside.' Kevin opens the door next to the coffee shop that takes him to the empty office. Kevin knows the owner of the coffee shop and sometimes uses his place for private meetings.

'Now spill the beans. I don't have whole day' Kevin waits for his response impatiently.

'OK, so what I am about to tell you is really big so you will be happy. The woman that destroyed your apprehension of the drug lord years ago is now out and she is making a real mess out of things'. The informer crosses his arms and gives Kevin the winning smirk. However, his boss doesn't react the way that he was expecting.

'Are you telling me that your big news and my reason to walk in this storm is for you to tell me that Kate is out of prison? The same Kate that I have PUT in there in the first place!! Are you FREAKING kidding me? I know how many years she got and I know that she was released. I knew when she will be out of prison before she even knew it, you IDIOT!' Kevin screams madly. There is a small kitchen cabinet on the left side of the room where the employees can make coffee or other drinks. Kevin moves there and takes a glass out of the cupboard. He pours himself a little glass of water and takes a sip, facing the kitchen sink. He knows that his informer is now sweating with fear which suits him well.

'You know that I have gun and cuffs with me at all time right?' Without giving the boy the chance to reply Kevin continues. 'You should also know that I don't pay you for an echo but for brand-new information. Since you are not complying with the rules of our agreement I can only take you back where you belong.' Kevin takes out the handcuffs from his belt and move towards his victim.

'Wait, there is something else. We're on the brink of war!!' The informer backs up and moves towards the wall, trying to avoid being taken back to prison.

'War? Why- - because of her? 'Kevin laughs thinking that the whole thing is just a joke. The strongest drug gang in the area and they are about to get to war because of one annoying little woman. That just doesn't make sense.

'Kate is like a catalyst. She is snooping around and making everybody do things which are not good for the business. All the fighting and arguing about which side she is on is becoming problem for the underworld. We cannot work proficiently if there is somebody always behind our backs trying to get us on our knees. Plus there is still that division of groups. Some people still believe that Kate is one of them as she kept her mouth shut during all these years. However, there are also people that blame her for everything that happened that day and for the death of Boss.' Informer sees that this information got Kevin's attention and mentally clap himself on the back for quick thinking.

'So she is a problem for me and also problem for you.' Kevin put his cuffs back and hands his informer a secure phone that cannot be traced to him.

'I need her gone and your people need her gone. I think it is time for you to make some calls.' Kevin holds the phone in front of the boy who only stares at it worryingly.

'I am not sure what you are proposing but I am not --!!'

'TAKE THE PHONE!!!!' The informer shockingly

takes the mobile and dials the number.

Chapter 22

At the end of the Sorreno Street is the club I was looking for AMARETO. It used to be owned by one of the dealers that I worked for while I was undercover. Now it belongs to Ralph, a drug addict with no conscience. The SECURITY GUY is new but seem to be more qualified that the last one. Or maybe they still didn't have change to get fond of their favourite drug, heroin. It is highly addictive and the moment person start feeling the need for more he would do anything to get it. Even kill.

The security guy looks at me suspiciously. There are not many women that want to get inside the joint without having male company. However, my dress code might make him feel like I am here for more than pleasure. This evening I am wearing tight grey jeans, black t-shirt and quite feminine shoes with heels. High enough to look sexy but not enough to get in my way. I unzip my leather jacket and he can see a gun sticking from my belt. I hope the rules are still same. Person with gun means business and is usually here for business. I pass the line of people hoping to get in. The noises of disapproval can be heard but nobody confront me knowing that it might be dangerous to do so.

Inside I try to adjust my vision to the darkness. The club is packed but no too much to be illegal. Usually in this kind of places the management tried to play by law as they don't want any uninvited guest. I pass the pinball tables, slot machines, car games and other beeping machines before I get to an arcade passage that divides the VIP or rather, 'business area' from 'economic area'. I am surprised that I am able to get in without anybody checking me out. I look around and see the owner and the person I am looking for waving me in. Ralf did change quite a lot from homeless, weak man I met years ago. It makes me wonder how he managed to get money to buy this whole. I do suspect that they needed a puppet to keep this waste of club going and who is better than somebody like a weak, uneducated and not to mention strongly manipulative addict such as Ralph.

I moved towards him observing his arrogant face. He knows this time he has got the power to kill me with the wave on his hand.

'Excuse me. What would you like to drink?' The waitress approaches me before I reach the table. The girl is a pretty, petite brunette with short hair. The haircut is very boyish but it really suits her together with her tight leather trousers and white vest. However, she also looks underage which is something that I will mention to Gina later to see if there is not some kind of trafficking going on in this place.

'Just double straight vodka, on the rocks.' Without giving the girl a second glance I sit opposite to Ralph. Finally I can see what money did for me. His teeth were fixed by some miraculous worker, his wardrobe change dramatically too but otherwise he remained that same white little skinny man.

'Kate, Kate, Kate - - Everybody is talking about you these past few days.'

'I feel flattered. That explain why you were expecting me today.'

'OK, so here you have me, now let's make it as short as possible.' Ralph takes a sip of his drink and indicates to the waitress to bring him another one.

'Man with a strong appetite. Before you were only a little druggie. Make sure that you don't get another addiction that you will have to deal with in your old age.' I can see that I upset him with my remark as he straightens his black suit.

'Don't be rude. I allowed you into my heaven and you should respect me now.' Ralph makes sure that I see his bodyguards standing close by.

'Get off your high horse. I am not here to fight you but I do need some information about recent killings.' I take the picture from my wallet and pass it to him. 'Also I need to know if you saw this girl in the last month.'

'I know lots of things. I even know that there is a cop in the house that was willing to sacrifice five years of her life in order to keep a cover. This is where my money is and I am always sure about my bets so I never gamble little amounts.' Now I understand how Ralph got this place. He won it in the bet. The last owner was a gambling ass and it looks like he lost everything. Ralph uses my contemplation of what he said to look at the picture.

'Hmm, you two are like two pieces of same cake. Cutie,' Ralph passes the picture back to me. 'However I do have to disappoint you. I don't know anything about the killer nor the woman on the picture. Now if you excuse me I do have to go back to my party.' Ralph stands up and takes his drink.

'Ralph, wait! Is there some kind of deal that we can do together in return for your cooperation?' I know that I am becoming desperate but it looks like nobody want to give me any clue or hints that would help me to find Karoline. The longer Karoline is missing the greater chance that she might not be alive anymore. That would lead to Suzy growing up without a mother. That is something that I won't let happen even if I have to beg. Ralph looks back at me with a raise eyebrow and I understand what kind of deal he has in mind.

'That is not what I meant. I am talking about business deal here.'

'Well, however appealing your proposal is I still have to stay behind my previous answer. We are not involved in any of the things that are now happening and thus there is nothing that I can offer to you as an exchange. So there is no business deal for you Kate. Go back where you came from.'

Ready to leave, I take my jacket and move towards the exit. Out of nowhere Gina appears in the door. My god if somebody recognised her, this place would become a war cone. I need to get her out of it as soon as possible. Quickly I move towards the stairs when Ralph moves behind me with his gorillas.

'But there is one piece of information I can give you.' I turn towards him with expectation. Suddenly a large hand takes me around the neck from behind, disabling my movement.

'What is this? I came here in peace,' I state calmly but inside I am boiling with confusion and fear.

'You see, Kate I might not help you with your problems but I happily help my people with theirs. You seem to be a distraction and many people wish you out of the picture.' I can only hope that Gina spotted me by now and is ready to act.

'Who is giving you order?' I enquire knowing well enough that I will not get answer but at least I will delay whatever is coming and allow Gina to get herself ready and call for backup.

'Wouldn't you like to know? - - hmm - - take her to the back and kill her - - quietly.'

I use all my power and step on the big guy's foot, grateful that I decided to wear the heels today. He screams in pain but that is nothing compared to what is coming his way. I turn and deliver a back hand punch and kick in his most favourable region. Ralph takes the gun out of his jacket and aims it at me but the crowd of people doesn't give him clear shot. I know that I have limited time before things will become ugly so I react quickly by kicking the table in front of me with all my power. That forces the man in front of me to fall backwards. The second bodyguard approaches me with his pocket knife. For a while we circle each other; the crowd of people disturbs my concentration. The bodyguard doesn't care about others. His goal is to kill me and if other fall during the process than so be it. I block his attack several times and with a quick round kick I disarm him. Second kick gets him to his knees. I take his hand and with a fast move, dislocate his shoulder.

'Freeze, Police!!!' Gina screams.

My god this girl needs some training. Why would she scream in the middle of the fight 'police'? I was hoping for something more subtle. Ralph swears loudly and turns to face Gina. He aims the gun this time at her and fires. That only create further mayhem and everybody around them start running for the exit. People are hitting each other and while others join the fight. Gina, still shocked from the bullet that barely missed her and starts running for cover as more bullets pass her. She takes a cover behind the table and I use the time to jump from the second floor of the club to the main area below. Ralph must saw me as he starts running down the stairs. Downstairs it is even more crowded. I unleash my anger in order to get pass them but nobody got hurt beyond bloody noses. Ralph manages to get past everybody and again we find ourselves face to face. Ralph tries to backhand me but with no success. I took one of the men fighting close to me and place him in front of me as a shield. Unfortunately for him he has to endure all the anger Ralph feels towards me at this moment. I look back and see Gina still behind the table trying to see if there is any way out of here. I push the guy in front of me on Ralph. The guy is bigger and squashes little Ralph below me. I know it won't keep him long so quickly I run towards Gina.

'Kate!!!!!' I hear Gina scream but cannot understand what is happening.

Tiny pieces of glasses keep flying all around the room, shattering into people legs as they run for their lives. The bullets from the gun fill up the floor and hit everything that stand in their way. Gina screams my name again and this time I see what makes her worried. Ralph is on his feet and aiming the gun straight at me. This time nobody is blocking his view. I turn and quickly jump behind the last crowed of people that try to push their way to the exit. I can hear Ralph swearing in frustration. I keep running around the crowd and once I am behind the Ralph I jump on the table behind him and dive on Ralph knocking him down. In the process I take his arm holding the gun and break it maliciously. The pain forces the hand to open and release the firing weapon. I kick it away and swiftly move again towards shaking Gina.

'I am so sorry Kate. I shouldn't have come here.' Gina tries to apologise thinking that her presence provoke this fight. How wrong she is. It looks like there is a price on my head.

'Now is no time for regrets.' I point the finger towards the exit just in front of them and then I take the gun from my waist. 'Cover me.'

'Ok let's do it on three, one....'

'Fuck three,' I interrupt Gina's mathematics lesson and leap from the cover. I only use the gun to fire in the air. There are still too many innocent people in here. The bullets are still fired all around me but luckily I manage to get outside and run across the street. Once out Gina emerges from the second exit on the other side of the building. I knew that my attempt to escape gives Gina enough time to run out of the building. I run towards her but all of the sudden the only thing I saw was light as a speeding car rams straight into me, forcing me to hit the ground. The last thing I saw before I lost my consciousness was the car hitting the lamp post and exploding.

Chapter 23

Kevin parks the car in front of the police station and sees the group of officers running out of the door. He wonders what all the chaos is about but is unable to get anyone to stop and answer his questions. One of the young cops is just placing the gun in his holster and starts sprinting towards his car where his partner is already waiting for him. Kevin stops him by grabbing his shoulder which almost resulted in the boy tripping, due to his slim size and still-developing muscles.

'What's happening boy? Why the rush?' Kevin looks down at him with stern expression.

'There were shots fired in the Amareto nightclub sir. It is real mess and many people are still inside.' The young officer said without taking any breath hoping that soon he will be able to get to car. He can see that his partner is now impatiently tapping the top of the wheel. It wouldn't be good for their last year review to have note attached to it indicating delay getting to the scenes.

'Are there any casualties?'

'We won't be sure till we get there but we are expecting that, yes sir.'

Kevin releases the boy who straightaway gets moving. Kevin faces all the cars that are now on the way to the club and small smile creeps on his face.

'Well, well. What a nice evening this turn out to be.'

With the spring in his steps Kevin gets inside the station.

#

Meanwhile Gina finds her way back to her office. She sits with a loud bang and places her head on the table hoping that it would somehow help her to concentrate. So many things happened in such a short time and it seems like now are things even more complicated. Nothing makes sense anymore. Gina opens the file in front of her and get to work. It will be morning soon anyway so no reason to go home now.

After couple of hours of putting together different pieces of puzzles Gina takes her wallet and goes to the buffet to get a sandwich. Being tired is one thing but being hungry and tired is another. After she purchased her lunch Gina decides to go to the roof. Nobody uses that area for anything other than smoking and usually early in the morning the place is empty. It's the perfect place to think of how to get Kate out of this mess.

Gina stares over the edge and take her puff of cigarette. It is interesting how quickly can thing change in life. People that she trusted are now considered to be dirty and her life is filled with suspiciousness, anger and revenge.

'I must say this is a great place for lunch. How is it that I have never eaten here?' Kevin stands behind Gina with smile on his face and Coke in his hand. Gina is startled and drops the cigarette that she was holding. With childish anger she turns to face Kevin.

'My god!!!! Do you always have to sneak up on me?' Gina holds her chest as her heartbeat is slowly getting back to normal.

'Sorry about that. Must be my training,' Kevin smiles with charm.

'Must be. I am off now. Just finished my lunch,' Gina starts walking towards the door.

'Do you want to hear big news?' Kevin asks gently before Gina makes even one step away from him. Not waiting for her response Kevin continues, 'Kate Summers was released from prison. She is somebody that used to be really big here once. I know it must be really confusing for you. We don't really talk about her anymore,'

'Why are you telling me this?' Gina asks knowing that she is getting into dangerous area. There is no proof that Kevin is not in some way involved in all of this.

'Apparently, she was the reason behind the fight that happened two days ago in Kenny's bar and also shooting yesterday. Lots of people were injured and died but she wasn't found at the scene. We are all looking for her though. It looks like Kate continued her rampage. Seems like prison didn't help her to rehabilitate- - - This could be the way out of this mess for us. I mean the media is killing us because of serial killer case. It is now too long and we need to show public that they can trust us and that we are able to protect them even if the person that we put in front of them might be not solely responsible,' Kevin states calmly as if Kate's life had no meaning for him.

'Kate Summers was in prison for five years and there is no –' Gina stops talking as she realised that she just uncovered her knowledge of Kate.

'Well, well, well. You must have been doing some extra homework. I have never mentioned to you how long Kate was in prison for.' Kevin moves closer to Gina in order to intimidate her into revealing what more does she knows. Gina tilts her head up and is ready for the confrontation that is about to happen.

'I am only doing my job. People have started to walk around the offices whispering. It was driving me insane so I had a little chat around with people and Kate's name came out once or twice.'

'More like twenty times.' Kevin is now face to face with Gina who is fighting not to move back.

'I need to go now - - sir - - work is not going to do itself.'

Kevin smiles and nods, giving Gina permission to move away from him. He finally breaks the eye connection and walks out onto the rooftop chuckling. Gina looks behind her with a scared expression in her face. She saw something in Kevin's eyes that gave her goose bumps. It was as he was trying to get inside her brain and empty it of all the information that she has. Why does he care so much about my knowledge? There is something happening her and she is going to put her fingers on it even if she has to work for 24 hours a week. First things first though. Firstly, Kate has to be rescued.

Chapter 24

I had a terrible dream that somebody is beating me on the head. It is making me feel dizzy. Slowly I open my eyes but it takes couple of second before I get a clear view of people around me. I see an angry Ralph holding his arm that was put into a makeshift sling. Ok, so two things are quite clear. I am not dead and it looks like I am tied up in the dark basement with people that want to kill me. Means I might be dead soon. There is nothing around to help me. Even windows are covered with woods and the cracks between wood provide the light for the room. Ralph slowly empties everything from his pocket. He takes out the set of tweezers and kneels in front of me.

'You know - -for years I was trying to figure out ways to inflict pain without too much work. The experimentation with other scumbags such as you I found out that tearing someone's eyeball is the best way to get information that I need. You wouldn't believe how much people value their sight.' Ralph smiles as he slowly moves tweezers in front of my face. Just as he is about cut take his cut there is a noise outside of the door.

'Ralph!' A person that I thought I would never see again entered the room.

'What the hell do you think you are doing?' Marshall passes Ralph's man and pushes him away from me. Marshall slowly takes my head and tilts it up.

'My god. I heard rumours but I still cannot believe that it is you. What are you doing here?' Marshall asks me impatiently but the warmth in his eyes cannot be missed.

'Again not the greeting that I was expecting.' I smile but it doesn't reach my eyes. I was hoping that at least Marshall would be happy to see me but obviously I was wrong.

'What did you expect? A hug? - - Do you understand the mess that you have caused and you are only out for couple of days. People around here have doubts about you but now odds aren't exactly in your favour.'

'And what did I do to make you doubt me?' I look him in the eyes showing all my feelings. Despair, anger and especially love. I have done so much for this man. Made sure that he is not on the list of people that needs to be arrested, covered his ass after every mistake he made and eventually helped him to escape the justice.

'Have you ever heard saying there is no smoke without fire?' Marshall asks the question that is clearly implying that my recent actions caused thick smoke around the mob world.

'I do have a slight idea what you are saying.' I divert my eyes to something else. I know if I keep looking at him I might start crying. Not because I am scared or weak but because I am tired of people betraying me all the time. So many people in my life are turning their backs to me. Nothing seems important anymore. Why do I go through it? It would be better if I died with others on that roof years ago. There is only one thing that keeps me silent. My sister. I need to find her so Suzy doesn't suffer the loss of her mother. I look back at Marshall with new determination.

'Well, I am sorry that you are so blinded. You like quotes. Well, I have one for you. The action speaks louder than the words. I would say my action during the trail is proof enough that I am not some dirty snake as you people tend to call me around here.'

Marshall is taken back by my anger. I know that even though he might trust me he will have to do something to keep the respect of his people.

'Why are you snooping around my clubs? Answer me this question and I might reconsider your punishment?' Marshall tries one last time to get me to co-operate but the years have changed me and I will no longer allow him to manipulate me.

'Don't make me laugh. You want to punish me for asking around about the whereabouts of my own sister? How far are you willing to go in order to save your face?'

Marshal hits me across the face angrily. I don't know what hurt more the impact or the knowledge that the person delivering the punch is somebody I used to love.

'Everybody leave now!!!' Marshall says calmly.

'What? No way. That bitch broke my arm and I want you to - - ' Ralph holds his ground, unwilling to move.

'If you don't listen to my orders than you will end up with so many bones broken on your body than

you will be unable to count them with your miserable education. Am I clear? Now leave - - - All of YOU!!!!!!'
All the men quickly move out of the door leaving me and Marshall finally alone.

Chapter 25

The moment that I was waiting for is here. Marshall stands in front of me but I don't know what to say.

'Is this really so necessary?' I point at the rope that is holding my feet and hands.

'I don't know anymore.' Marshall keeps walking up and down the room. 'You know that by attacking my own men I have created even bigger hole for myself. For years I was trying to become a good successor but now you back and everything else seems meaningless.'

'Do you trust me Marshall?'

'I am not certain if I can.'

'Is there anything that you are certain of? Come on, I am only asking you to give me a chance. I need to find out who is behind the killings and - - 'Marshall snaps and gets right in my face.

'So this is what this is all about. The killings.' Marshall backs off.

I can see that he is upset but don't know why. Did he really think that I came back because of him? I loved and maybe still love him but I never wanted to come back to this life. I wanted to start over with clean slate and unfortunate that future didn't include him.

'And what did you think? - - That I have come back her to declare my undying love to you. After you let me take all the blame and didn't even have guts to visit me once in prison. Don't be an idiot? The only reason I am here is to find out where Karoline is and who is behind the mob killings.'

'So you saying you don't love me anymore?' Marshall asks, bluntly dismissing everything else I was saying.

'What? Marshall you can't be serious. This isn't about us but about people dying around us.' This is not the time nor the place for this kind of conversation. I am not ready for it.'

'Fine, have it your way but why sudden concern about our well-being? You just said we let you down.'

'No, I said YOU let me down.' My words hurt Marshall but I cannot care less. He deserves it and more.

'Ok, still I don't know why you want to help us. But let me indulge you. You know that we don't kill our own people so it must be somebody from outside.'

'The problem is that they are no longer your people. There is a split happening in the organisation and you know it. It is bigger than you and you cannot control it. There are snake all around here trying to get you down. Maybe somebody thirsty for power is killing mobs to distract you.'

Marshall starts pacing around me as a caged animal. He knows that I am right but his hands are tied. Even more than mine.

'No,' I state quietly interrupting Marshall's thoughts.

'What?'

'No, I don't love you,' I whisper. Marshall glares at me. The noise behind the door is louder and it is obvious that soon the room will be full of angry mobsters.

'You don't mean anything to me. Not now, not ever!' I finished and the pain in his eyes made me feel better than I thought possible. Marshall delivers a second punch knocking me down with the chair. The impact breaks the chair and gives me chance to get out of restraints. Marshall is now aware that I tricked him in order get free.

'I forgot how clever you can be.' Marshall laughs. 'Now go and find out who is responsible for the death of my men.'

We both get ready for the fight as door to the room are broken down.

'Just like old times.' This time I have to smile at the Marshall's sentiment. Ralph together with the goons burst into the room. I use the broken chair's legs as weapon. Without any effort the first two men fall down as wood hit them across their heads. Marshall steps in front of me.

'Go Kate. Leave this to me. I didn't have a proper fight for a long time,' Marshall says and I can see a happy smile on his face as I move pass him. Ralph tries to stop me but only ends up with the broken nose.

'Son of a bitch!!!!!!' Ralph screams in pain.

Chapter 26

I barely manage to get to the door of my building before collapsing on the stairs. It is too cold to sleep here. I need to move before somebody notices me and alert police. Shakily I stand back up and get inside. Almost there.

'My God, are you ok?' Gina opens my door and rush towards me.

'I don't remember last time the door was open at my place and you weren't there.' I move passed her looking for something soft to fall on.

'I heard that there was another fight in the bar so I hoped maybe you got away.' Gina tries to help me but I shake her hands off. I need some time to get myself under control.

'Are you supposed to be the one that acts instead of waits?' I lie down on the couch and close my eyes. 'I need to rest. Had a busy couple of hours.'

#

I am back in my dreamscape enjoying some peace and quiet. This time there is no Marshall. I am alone in the field full of trees and animals. The noise of wind and birds makes me relaxed. I walk around the trees enjoying the feeling of wood under my hands. Everything is perfect but one thing. Something is tickling my left leg and the feeling irritates me. I scratch the spot but uncomfortable feeling return again. The trees disappear and I found myself back in the darkness. I open my eyes and looks down at the person that so annoyingly shortened my well-deserved sleep.

'What are you doing?' I ask Gina who is still absorbed in the tattoo analyses.

'Oh my god, you scared me. Sorry, I didn't know that you are up. Hope I didn't wake you up. I was just looking at your tattoo and trying to figure out the meaning of it.' Gina quickly stands up and take a step back, feeling embarrassed.

'Chill woman. I am only up for couple of seconds and yes it is because of your tickling mission. But it doesn't matter. I needed to wake up at some point anyway.' I try to sit up but all the bones in my body are against that idea. Gina comes to me with intention to help but after my recent brush off she is not sure if she can. I take a hold of her hand and slowly get myself in the sitting position.

'So?' I ask.

'So what?'

'Did you figure out the meaning of my tattoo?'

'No I didn't but it seems very interesting and mysterious just as you are. So I think it suits you.' Gina's honesty can be so endearing.

'I got one done as well years ago by my brother Harry.' Gina slides off the stripe of her shirt to reveal a small ink on her right top shoulder. Kate looks at the Greek symbol of hope. Gina covers her shoulder and sits down, defeated.

'Come on. Let's not do this again. Your brother didn't deserve what happened to him but life can be sometimes cruel and not everybody has the will power to face it and still uphold the rules. We all have both light and darkness inside of us and there is a very thin line that is dividing those two worlds. I always believe that by joining police work I would be on the side of light but instead of that I was throwing myself into undercover work every time I could just so I can be part of the darkness. Not sure what is says about me but I can tell you it doesn't make me a bad person. And the same can be said about your brother. Just because he was unable to resist the darkness doesn't make him bad, it only makes him human. We all have our reasons for our actions and we all can make mistakes. I am sure with time he would have return back to you and ask for help.' I wipe the tear from Gina eye.

'Thanks.' Gina moves away from me and get up to bring some water.

'You said that we all have some reasons. What are yours? Why did you decide to stay in prison and take all the blame on yourself?' Gina asks with curiosity.

I take a sip of the water and look at the blank spot behind Gina feeling myself being pull back to the time when everything started.

'Firstly, it wasn't so hard for me to fit into the group. I was young, wild and didn't like authority. Mobs like characteristics like this in their new recruits. I sold some dope for them and later on start asking for more and more opportunities to prove myself to them. Of course, everything was controlled by Adams and other detectives that were assigned to the mission. After a year I was a high profile member of the mafia and many people were scared of me. In their eyes, I was a woman without boundaries and no attachments. My profile said that my parents died when I was young and from a very young age I was moved from one home to another, getting into as much trouble as possible. There was nothing that could destroy my cover out there.' I take a deep breath and look at the frame picture on the table. 'Except her.'

Gina looks at the picture with confusion.

'I don't understand.' Gina keeps looking everywhere on the table thinking that maybe she missed something. I laugh at Gina's oblivious and continue with my story.

'One day I decided to meet Adams to give him some more information about the next hit that was about to happened during the night. That day I was not at home at all and missed a call from my sister telling me that she is getting on the plane to visit me. Can you imagine my surprise when I got a phone call from Marshall accusing me of playing on two sides? Karoline came to see me with her boyfriend at the time, JACK. Jack was a nice guy but he tended to hang around wrong people that were supplying him with light drugs. This wouldn't be such a big problem but during that time those little drug dealers were standing in the way of the underworld organisation. You see, street dealers kept the prices low to get larger clientele. Big bosses didn't like it.

'Wait! I am losing track of it all. What your sister has to do with the fact that Marshall thought you had betrayed them?' Gina asks unable to keep up.

'Karoline is my twin sister, Gina. Didn't you get it yet? This is not my place but hers. All the pictures around here are not of me but of Karoline with Suzy.'

Gina eyes widen with surprise. 'Oh my god, this all makes sense now.'

'Not really. Let me finish. Marshall was not alone when he spotted Karoline. There were couple of other boys with him and of course they told everything to the main boss. Everybody thought I had betrayed them so the hunt was on and in order for me to protect my sister I had to lie to them and say that it was me on the street that time. Otherwise, my sister would have been killed and my niece would have no mother and that is something I was not willing to take responsibility for.'

Gina stands up and starts pacing. 'Now it makes sense why you are so desperate to find Karoline. You think maybe somebody confused her with you and took their revenge?'

'I really don't know what to think. If they had found out that Karoline is my sister then I would know about it by now. They would look very surprised to see me walking the street and somebody would have spill the beans. Furthermore, Kenny knows about her so he would know what had happened.' I stop talking but my memories continue to play in front of me. There must be something that I have missed.

'I told Adams that I will arrange a meeting with underworld boss and use as a cover story that my association with street dealers was for their benefit to get closer to their suppliers. Than Adams will come with the team and arrest everybody including me so it doesn't look suspicious. To make sure that Karoline and Suzy are safe I had to remain incarcerated for as long as judge decided. That means that even now my cover is still intact but there are many people on the street that either don't trust me anymore.'

'Ok but that doesn't explain why you think the killings have anything to do with you and Karoline?' Gina asks carefully.

'Anything is possible. All those killings seem to be framing the mobs but from personal experience I know that mobs don't kill their own. Of course it could be somebody who is trying to prove himself or take over their turf. Karoline was living here and working full time to support herself and the child. Kenny was looking after them and making sure that nobody connects the dots. Karoline was no longer involved with Jack and without him she was not hanging in the places where she could be recognised. Plus most of the people that are currently working for underworld don't know about what happened as most of the old ones are either dead or in prison.'

Both Gina and I become quiet, trying to figure it all out. Now I know that Marshall is not involved and nobody seems to know who Karoline is.

'Come on Kate. Think! All of this is somehow connected with you. The killing started close to your release. You sister disappeared close to your release. There must be something. Can you think of anybody that holds grudge against the mobs and you personally?'

I try to think but nothing is coming my way. The people that hate me are mostly criminals and they wouldn't wait for my return to commit crimes. Again I think of the undercover case and something comes to my mind that takes my breath away.

'Oh my god. I cannot believe I forgot about him.'

'What is it?' Gina says with anticipation.

'There is one person that fit the character of the revenge killer. He was my partner in the force when I started. Together we led every raid and busted many criminals on the street. Unfortunately, my task didn't allow me to tell him that I went undercover so the night when I was arrested he was one of the officers on the scene. The whole scenario had to be played to the dot so to avoid mistakes I made him believe that I betrayed him and everything we were fighting for. Never heard about him after that but now when I am thinking about it he was the one that lost the most from my arrest. He was about to be promoted for all his hard work to chief detective. I do believe that my arrest must have put delay to his work progress.' This is so unreal. The answer was so close to me and I didn't even think about it. If I am right this case is solved.

'What was the name of the guy? Maybe I know him.' Gina sits, waiting for my response.

'His name is Kevin Collins.'

'Oh shit!' Gina's eyes widen with realisation.

Chapter 27

The night is filled up by sirens as the police cars rush through the dark street of the city. The phone call was received by one of the passer-by that saw a person with a gun walking into the petrol station. There is no exact description of the suspect and no indication of what is his intention. The cars stopped, cops open the door and take the cover behind their vehicles. One of the cops took an alert megaphone, ready to negotiate with the person inside. So far it looks as there is only the suspect and cashier inside.

'Ok, this is Officer Kay and I am here to help you. Don't do anything that you will regret later. I am giving you now a chance to come out with your hands in the air.' Kay yells with confidence as he was trained. The only way to negotiate with criminals is by understanding and empathy.

The door to the petrol station slowly open and without further encouragement a person emerges wearing a black jumper and black trousers. The suspect has a hood on the head so it is difficult to see the appearance of the person who holds the gun in the left hand.

'Drop the gun!'

A suspect slowly takes off the hood from the head and to everyone surprise it is their ex- officer, Kate that is hidden underneath. I smile and casually get on my knees. In the process I drop the gun to the floor and put my hands in the air. The surrender procedure was done exactly by the book and without any resistance from my side. This needs to be smooth.

Officers at the scene seems to be surprised by my fast submission but don't question it too long. I believe that there must be some kind of price in the form of promotion waiting for person that will bring me in. Key approaches me, takes the gun from the floor and put the handcuffs on my hands. 'What the hell happened to you Kate? You used to be one of us.' Key says with hatred in his voice.

'You don't know what you are talking about little boy. Life is not as black and white as you might think.' I say as he leads me to the car and takes me to the exact place I want to be.

#

I sit patiently in the middle of the interrogation room. There is only table and one chair in the whole room that is covered with white wallpaper. On the left side of the room is the mirror that gives people from other side view of what is happening during the questioning. I have never anticipated that I will be one day sitting in the same room where I brought all the scumbags and attempted to get a confession out of them. This is what happened when dark forces entice you and make you unaware of the danger you getting yourself into.

Captain Adams get inside the room and looks at me as I am some kind of psycho. It is quite amusing to see such a composed man to be so frustrated. I should do it more often just for the sake of fun.

'Hello, nice to see you again!'

'What the hell are you doing going into the petrol station with the gun? Despite what you think you are not above the law.' Adams leans against the table, furious with my calm demeanour. He is not the reason why I came here and for now I am not sure if I can trust him with my suspicious. The comment about the law didn't get missed by me. It is interesting how quickly people can forget the past.

'Are you kidding me? I have spent years in prison for a crime that wasn't even a crime. I was working for you and because of me you managed to catch the biggest fish in the mob world. Instead of thank you I had to go to prison so please can you spare me the lecture.' I feel like throwing something at him for such an outrageous statement. It is not enough that I have my sister missing and everybody wants to kill me but now I need to deal with ungratefulness.

'I do value what you did but it was your choice to remain undercover even during the time of the court so I had no way to protect you. It was your decision.'

I am aware of the truthfulness of what Adams is saying but still I am unwilling to admit it. Maybe I should have fought more to try to get out of it without losing so many precious years. Maybe I would have different life now, possibly even a husband and child. I look back at the mirror and wonder who is standing behind it. Suddenly the door to the investigation room opens again and Kevin barges in, looking unhappy. Finally, let the show begin.

Chapter 28

'Why she is being treated with the golden gloves. She had committed an armed robbery and should be in the prison cell awaiting her punishment.' Kevin says to Adams; however, his eyes have not strayed from mine.

'I know that detective, and shall I remind you that I am your boss and you have just crossed the line.' Adams is furious with Kevin's disobedience but knows that Kevin is right. He is not being objective and if he wants to follow the rules he needs to leave me alone with my ex-partner so I can be properly question.

'I will let you continue this interrogation but you behaviour today will be still discuss at later stage.' Adams leaves the room promptly.

'What do you want?'

I like the way Kevin can get straight to the point. But I am shall allow him to press me to the wall quickly. I need time so Gina can get some evidence for me.

'You know just the fact you are asking me makes me wonder what YOU are hiding?' I slightly laugh just to irritate him a little bit.

'I don't know what you are talking about. I have nothing to hide but you on the other hand are playing with fire considering your recent behaviour.' Again Kevin doesn't realise how predictable he is. He always had problem with females that are dominant and wiser than him. Even know he is fidgeting and moving around the room as some kind of lost puppy instead of sitting down and showing me who is the boss in this situation.

'What are you referring to? The fact that I committed armed robbery or that I am trying to figure out why such a decorated detective is killing mobsters in his free time?' This time it is me that is going straight to the point. Kevin is not following the interrogation procedure and thus he must know that I am here for a reason. The room become deadly silent. I wait for the verbal attack, denial or even his accusation of my involvement. But nothing happened. Kevin just looks at me for a while and suddenly starts laughing.

'Oh Kate you are good. Very good. But still not good enough,' Kevin continues to laughing and that starts to make me anxious. Maybe I was wrong coming here and having this confrontation. Kevin is a person that I used to know for many years but after everything that happened he must have changed and maybe I don't know the scale of his insanity.

'You really think that I am so stupid as to leave incriminating objects around for you to find? Is this why you are here? To get Adams to do your dirty work and dig something from my record or is it your little sidekick on the mission to recover something from my flat? I hope the years in the prison didn't make you forget that there are certain steps and rules you need to follow in order to use your evidence in the court of justice.' Marshall snares at me with disgust.

'Oh I am well aware of that. But you must have lost the memory of who I am. Rule, regulation and law is something that I never properly follow but I still managed to get results.' I can see now anger in Kevin's eyes and I am ready for the impact of his fist. Instead of that he kicks the chair from under me and threw me with all his power against the wall.

'Kevin, think about what you doing. There is still a chance for you to get out of it intact. I can protect you. You know that I have people in higher places and I can ensure that things will disappear. Just tell me what you have done!!!!?' I can feel as the breath is becoming shorter as Kevin increases his strong hold around my neck but I have to remain conscious to find out the truth. 'Tell me! Tell me what did you do to my sister!!!?' Finally I said the question I am desperate to get an answer to. Marshall releases me from his grasp. The look in his eyes devastates me. He is confused which means he knows nothing about Karoline.

'What do you mean your sister? Why should I care about her in the first place? It is enough to have one Summers on my hands, I don't need another one.' Kevin starts kicking me in the stomach but without having my arms released from the handcuffs I am unable to protect myself. I know, though that if I don't escape now that he might kill me. I manage to find the leg of the chair that falls next to me and use my strength to break it against Kevin's head. I know that the hit was not strong but it provides me with opening to get on my feet and run towards the door that were now open as one of the officer rushes in after he hears disturbing noise from the room. I push him with my shoulder against the wall and take a hold of the keys that he had hanging on his belt.

I can hear Kevin shouting at the officers to get me but I know this building as my own home and know exactly how to get out of here. I continue running towards the security door that is now without any protection as everybody is concentrating on Kevin's commands. I close the door behind me and punch the code to the door locking it. It is funny how people become comfortable at their job and forget to change something some as sensitive as password of secure building. I continue running towards the parking door. I only stop for a second to unlock the handcuffs.

Kevin's men now open the door and are in the strong pursuit behind me but they are not fast enough as I am already sitting in one of the police cars and moving down the street. This visit was not what I was expecting but at least now I know who is responsible for the death of Gina's brother Henry and that serial killer case and Karoline's disappearance are not connected.

Chapter 29

Kevin sits at the table still wondering how Kate slipped through his fingers so smartly. Something caught his attention though. What did she mean by asking him where was her sister. There is no reason for him to know information like that. He knows that Kate has a sister but she barely mentioned her during the rides together and he was never really interested to find out more. They were friendly with each other and sometimes even exchange some personal information but they were both very professional and value they privacy. Kevin's thought were interrupted by the phone call.

'Hello, Collins speaking.'

'Come to my office right now!' Adams's voice was full of anger just as Kevin expected. He hung up the phone with all his power. This is the last thing that he wanted to be dealing with right now.

Kevin stands up and left his office that is a mess. Uncaringly Kevin knocks on Adams door that are just two doors from his ones and get immediate approval to get in.

'Can you explain to me what the hell happened in there? My whole office is completely out of order and nobody is doing their jobs besides looking for a woman that is undercover officer. Don't we have other things that we need to deal with such as murder on the loose?' Adams throws questions at

Kevin without even giving him slight chance to respond. 'That woman was responsible for all the crucial arrests that occurred during the first three years of her undercover work. Every intel came from her and now is the time for us to protect and help her and not to go against her for some kind of petty crime.'

Kevin sits down at the table cockily. He is not even slightly surprised that Adams is taking it so personally. It was expected, as he had a very soft spot for Kate since the commencement of her work in law enforcement. Maybe it is the fact that she is in the age of his daughter.

'I thought it was you who said to me that there is nobody above the law and now you saying that her crimes are petty. Should I remind you that she committed arm robbery in the public place and endanger civilians in the process.'

Adams understands what Kevin is saying but still he feels like they are all being too harsh at her. It is time to clear the Kate's name and make her be a hero that she deserved to be from the onset.

'Kevin, there is something you don't know. Kate didn't betray us as you were led to believe. She was undercover the whole time but because of the sensitivity of the case we had to make sure that there are no links that can in some way connect her to us. The only people that knew that she was working with us were me and chosen people from NYPD narcotic division. I am sorry but she couldn't even tell you about it.'

Kevin keeps staring at Adams without blinking. The statement didn't come as a surprise to him. He knew that Kate wasn't able to become criminal in a matter of day so he did some of his own digging years ago and find out about so called secret operation. The fact is she still betrayed him. He was for years working with her when no men wanted to have anything to do with her. But instead of trusting him she went behind his back. She knew in advance about every deal, every transaction and she not once tried to point him to the right direction. The last bust was the last straw for him. The way she was looking at the man on that roof spoke the volume. She loved him and was willing to fall for him. How is it possible that the majority of the people from that night were arrested and prosecuted but he was able to get out of it without any charges?

'That doesn't change anything for me. As my partner she betrayed me. Everybody should be responsible for their action. I am fed up with people not paying for wrong doings because it is convenient'.

'Kevin, this is not out of convenience. She is innocent and it is time for the world to hear the whole truth.

Abruptly, Kevin leaps from the table towards the surprised Captain Adams and wrap his tie around his neck. Adams is struggling but the old age and damaged health cannot be compare with the power of a man as strong as Kevin. Slowly Adams starts losing his strength and falls to the ground. Kevin hands turns as he follows Adams to the floor not losing the contact with him for one second. The anger that he felt while Adams was justifying Kate's behaviour was slowly diminishing. Adams's eyes are fixed at Kevin as he takes his last breath.

'Well sir, I cannot allow you to clear your consciousness now when finally I am were I have always wanted to be. You know - - this time Kate will take the fall for me. If she is so happy to spend time in prison for criminals than she can do it for her great partner. And then I will get my promotion as I will be the one bringing her to justice.' Kevin washes his hands while he talks and look in the mirror to ensure that he looks as distraught by this tragedy as possible. Today is a day when a great man left us due to his weak heart. Kevin smiles and moves towards the phone on the table.

Chapter 30

I am wondering while I am sitting in the car how things could turn out the way they did in such a short time. I trusted Kevin while we were working together. He was my closest friend and now he is my worst enemy. He still might be the one that is responsible for what happened to Karoline. Maybe he doesn't know her but he has started the events that could led bad people to her. I need to find out if Gina found any evidence in Kevin's place that would implicate him in the crimes against mobs. I take the phone and dial the number. There is a response shortly.

'Gina, can you hear me?' There is some kind of weird noise in the background. Sound as if somebody is crying.

'Yes, I am fine. Are you ok?' Gina responds.

'Gina, what the hell is wrong? I can barely hear you. Did you find something that connects him to the murders?' I am getting slowly very frustrated with this girl. There is always something emotionally wrong with her. She needs to pull it together if she wants to work in this profession.

'No, I found nothing. His place is completely ordinary and clean. Nothing that can connect him to what is happening here. But there is something else you should know.' Gina becomes even more distraught and her voice is cracking as she is trying to say next sentence. 'I just got a phone call from fellow officer. He said that Adams died couple of minutes ago of a heart attack.'

I am shocked with the news. I was with Adams just seconds ago and even though he didn't look the healthiest he was still ok. What the hell happened in such a short period of time? Maybe stress got to him. These last couple of days were just crazy and he wasn't the youngest guy to handle such a pressure.

'Kate, did you hear me?' Gina asks, worrying.

'Yes, I heard. How that could have happened so suddenly? Are you ok?' I can hear that Gina is not handling the situation well but hopefully she will be able to pull through. Adams was a special person and his dead is very unfortunate but the investigation needs to continue. We are so close now.

'I am fine. It is just too much but I will be ok. He was just discussing with Kevin your escape when it happened,' Gina blows her nose.

Kevin was with Adams during his heart attack. Suddenly an unfortunate accident becomes more obvious one. Adams must have told him about my involvement with mobs or something that tick him off. Now I don't believe that Adams just collapsed after stressful day. It is not time to tell Gina that I think Kevin is responsible for the murder of her brother and now her boss. She needs to clear her head and look at the bigger picture in this whole scenario.

'Ok listen, I need to pop in to the flat. Need to take some paper and I will meet you in the coffee shop across from your apartment. I will tell you everything then.' I hang up before Gina could reply.

Suddenly, the glass of my left car window shattered and hit me straight in the face. A hand reaches inside of the car and tries to pull me out. I have no idea what is happening but instead of wasting time I turn the key and start the engine of the car. My face is still on the other seat of the car so just slightly I touch the wheel and turn it to the left as the car moves from the spot. However, the intruder is still holding the part of my jacket so I am dragging him behind me for couple of seconds. The speed of the car slowly increases. I turn back and see that there are three different police cars now in my pursued and the man that attacked me is now lying on the street. It is Kevin Collins. I could see in the rear-view mirror as he stands up and runs towards his car.

Kevin keeps his eye on me as he manoeuvres his car through the traffic. There is no way for me to escape if I remain on the main road so I turn to the right to the narrow street. The pursuing cops split up. Two of them, including Kevin stay behind me and other two are trying to stop me by blocking the road on the other side. I speed up even more. I am lucky that it is a work day and all the children are at school otherwise I would be in the big trouble. Kevin also speeding up and hits the back of my car with his front couple of times which only helps me to move faster. I need to get to the other side of the narrow street before other cars get to another side of the street.

The street leads to a steep embankment. I look back trying to figure out which car out of five is Kevin's but it is difficult to determine it from such a distance. I look back in front and avoid colliding with the bus full of people.

'Where do you thinking you are going Kate? There is no way out of here.'

It is Kevin talking into the radio. I completely forgot I am sitting in the police car. I keep my one hand on the wheel and pick the hand radio with the other as other officers start firing at me from their guns.

'Kevin, tell your men to stop firing. There are too many civilians!!' I yelled into the radio but there is no response. Of course Kevin doesn't give a damn if somebody will get injured or not as long as he gets me. I throw the radio out of the window.

One officer manages to get his car next to me and aim the gun at my broken window. I ram the car with all the power before he can pull the trigger and it send his car flying through a shop window. Another police car is impacted and hits the wall next to the other car. There are only three cars reminding that are still in the close proximity to me. I drive again to the alleyway and all three cars are straight behind me. I sharply turn the car to another street and another and another till I see offshoot garage driveways and reverse into it. I hide the car from the view and wait till all the police cars pass me. I know this city better that Kevin could ever know. Years working undercover gave me opportunity to be in almost every dark allies and empty factories that exist in this city. Slowly I come back into the road and re-join the traffic. I can see in the distance Kevin and other officers rushing through the road trying to find out where I am. I move my car slowly towards the petrol station and get out before they see me.

Things didn't turn the way I expected. Too many people have been wounded or killed because of her need to get justice for people that might not even deserve it. They were criminals after all responsible for many deaths. Maybe not personally but they were the one that addicted young and innocent people to lethal drugs that led them to their ultimate ending. I should have maybe let it go and concentrate on Karoline only. Suzy will be coming home soon and I don't even know what to tell her. I need help desperately and there is only one person that can provide it for me. I am still walking on the empty streets and now with the destination on my mind I start slowly running towards it. People around me are unaware of what is happening in their neighbourhood. The life is just a joke. You think that you are strong enough and capable enough to protect yourself from the darkness that lurk within it but one wrong step, wrong decision and wrong action can completely destroy everything that you have been working for your whole life.

Chapter 31

Again I found myself in front of Kenny's home. He was always there for me when I needed him in the past and I believe that even now he will not disappoint me. I don't wait for an invitation and open the door. It doesn't look as anybody is at home but suddenly somebody closes the door behind me. I sharply turn and see Marshall standing there. He is handsome as always, wearing a dark blazer and slightly lighter shirt. However, this time Marshall is not as groomed as usual. His hairs are all around and it looks like he hasn't eaten or slept for a while.

'You know, Kate it is not nice to be doing all the mayhem around the city when people are trying to lead a normal life.' Marshall doesn't take his eyes off of me. He moves closer so I can almost feel his body on my skin. Don't take me wrong. I am a person that knows how to keep composure but years in the feminine presence can make people feel a bit anxious when they are around somebody like Marshall. 'You are responsible for many casualties today and because people taken you as one of us we have police, FBI and NYPD breathing on our neck. – And I am sure you know that we don't like that.'

'I don't know what you want me to say. I do tend to be popular.' It is time to return the favour so I move even closer to him. He had always weakness for me just like I had always weakness for him. So let's see if the sparks are still flying between us. I slowly touch his arm and move my index finger from the upper

150

part of his shoulder to the lower. I can feel him breathing heavily but before I could move one step further he retreats.

'I always thought that I am a good judge of character but based on recent events and what I had found out from Marshall I think I was wrong.'

Kenny has been standing behind me the whole time. I never knew I can get so easily distracted.

'What are you talking about Kenny? I have never lied to you.' I feel the need to protect myself. Yes it is true that I was working undercover but I was very specific with my instructions. I was making sure that Kenny is always protected him by making him my Intel without his knowledge. It was the only way I could keep him out of the harm way.

'So you mean you have never implanted yourself within the organisation as one of us in order to get an access to sensitive and confidential information about our activities?'

Wow, this is the first time that Kenny said so many words in one go. If the situation wasn't so serious I would have to applaud him. However, this time I have to keep my cool. Obviously Marshall must have told Kenny things about me that make him doubt me. I am not sure what the right course of action is at this moment. He knows about Karoline and to be honest I am quite surprise that it took him so long to put together the whole puzzle. I think the best defence in this situation is no defence. Things got already way too far.

'We all have our purpose in this world. I decided to be protector of innocent and I was only doing my job.

But Kenny, I have never lied to you.'

Kenny starts laughing but his eyes remained cold and still fixed at me.

'I lie to you about my profession but I have never lied to you about my feelings and who I am inside.'

'Because of you many of my friends died and went to prison and you are telling me that you are my friend! Are you freaking kidding me?!!!'

Kenny rushes towards me, ready to punch the living hell out of me. I didn't even raise my hands. I know that he feels betrayed and that I don't deserve his forgiveness for what I have done. People that died because of me were his family and even though they belong to the black sheep they were still important to him. He is just about to strike his first punch when Marshall pulls me behind him.

'Calm down man, ok. This is neither the time nor the place. Everybody is looking for us now. Ralph is now in common and she is more valuable to us alive and kicking than dead and motionless.'

Kenny sneers at Marshall but he also knows that he is right. Kenny's hands are still tightly clenched by his side when the phone rings. Kenny picks up the phone without saying a word. Whoever is on the other side must know that Kenny is listening as Kenny's eyes widen once he hears the news. Straight after that he hangs up and pick up the jacket from the chair.

'I have to go. I want two of you out of here before I am back.' This was Kenny's last sentence before he banged door behind him.

Now it was just me and Marshall alone in the room which is not good at all. I am still not ready to have sensitive chat with him but I know that I cannot wait any longer.

'It is Kevin. Detective Kevin Collins who is responsible for all the deaths.' I said the first thing that came to my mind.

Chapter 32

'What?' Marshall asks me, shocked. I think he didn't expect that the first thing that I will say to him will be that one of my own is walking the streets and killing their people. But as I mentioned before I was never good with sensitive chats.

'He is doing it as some kind of revenge for my betrayal. He never knew about my assignment so he thinks that I turned my back on him and join you. I think he is mentally unstable and ready to punish everybody who stands between him and so-called justice'.

'Was he wrong? Who are you, Kate? Are you a detective or are you just a regular woman at this moment?'

I open my month to give Marshall the answer that would make him hate me but somehow the words didn't come out. I am not sure who I am anymore. I feel so confused with everything. Doesn't matter if what I am doing is right or wrong there is still somebody who is trying to kill me. There are always people suffering doesn't matter what decisions I make. When I was working undercover I had to endanger my whole family and people that I worked with. Now the same people are killing the one that I have learnt to love and trust. World is so difficult sometimes. Why things cannot be clearer and less complicated. I would love to one day to wake up and know exactly who I am, where I am going and what I am doing. It is not the case though and I will have to finally learn to live with it. But now at this moment I only want to be a regular woman that desires a regular man. I move closer to Marshall who is still passionately waiting for my next step. Slowly I push him against the wall and kiss him with all the passion and emotion that I can find within myself. He doesn't wait long and kiss me back. His hands are moving from my shoulder to my lower body and for a split second I feel like his touch is everywhere. He lightly pushes me backwards and towards the bedroom. Somehow I believe that an upcoming moment of desire will be the most honest thing that I have done since my imprisonment and I will not let anybody to destroy it. I close the door with my foot, ready to finally have my sensitive chat but without any words exchanged.

#

I wasn't expecting that it would happen but it did and it felt amazing. For a while, it was as old times. Again, I am lying in his arms, feeling content and happy. I move my head closer to his and place my arms slowly around his chest.

'It is either my heart still beating twice the speed or someone's phone is buzzing.' Marshall still talks with the sleeping voice. My mobile is on the floor together with my trousers. I reluctantly disengage myself from him and remove the irritating tool from my pocket. There are three missed calls and one message from Gina. Wow, people can become extremely oblivious to other things when they are having fun. And we did have some serious fun for an hour.

There is no voice message, just a text that says: "We need to meet now. It is urgent. Watch news". I look around the room and in the corner I saw the remote from the little TV that is on the nightstand. I switch the TV on and look for the 24 hours news channel.

The news is filled up by cops and in the middle of it all is Marshall giving a speech. I increase the volume to hear what is being said but I can already feel how fear is embracing me as I see parametric caring out of Karoline's block two black bags with dead bodies.

NEWS: Kevin's statement

My name is Detective Collins at Fairland Avenue. I cannot give you a lot of information as yet. First, we need three victims to be identified by their family. However, the suspect is under arrest and we are confident that in couple of hours we can confirm both the decease identities and the name of the killers. The last thing I can say is that after all the paper work is finished I will have some big news relating not only to this incident but also to the mob killer case. This is our break through and I am happy that the nightmare is coming to the end. Thank you and please at this point don't ask any further questions as I will not be able to give you any specific answers.

I am still sitting on the bed but this time Marshall has his strong hands around me.

'What do you think all this means?'

'I don't know but I am worried. If Kevin is so giddy it means that we are in a lot of trouble.' I am still staring at the screen. Who is in that bag and why Kevin is saying that everything will come to the light soon. He is the killer, so for him saying that mob killer case will be uncover soon means that he managed to find a way to frame somebody else. I wrote a text to Gina that I will meet her in twenty minutes in the alleyway close to the police HQ. It is shame that this special moment was destroyed so quickly but it is better this way. No reason to get deeper into something that will never survive.

'Marshall, you go back to your place and try to find out how many people are still working for you and how many decided to follow Ralph. I think intervention is in order. I need to go and meet Gina.' I pick all my clothes and quickly put them on. It doesn't take me long as I am use to work under pressure. In the prison I didn't have the comfort of the time. Once the alarm went on we only had couple of seconds to make sure everything is tidy and we are ready for the morning count.

'Ok but you be careful and I will see you soon,' Marshal says to my back as I closed the door and move swiftly toward the car.

Chapter 33

I keep daydreaming about my steaming moment with Marshall while I am driving through the street. There is no way to say if this will lead somewhere but odds are strongly against us. I cannot get sucked into the world of crime again just so I can keep my relationship with Marshall. Firstly, there is no way to think of it as a relationship just yet and risk is too high. Secondly I still don't know what Marshall wants. The best thing to do at the moment is to concentrate on what is happening with the mob turf takeover and Kevin. Something seems odd about what I saw in the news and somehow I do suspect that the events that occurred during the last couple of hours will shape my future in the way that I will surprise even me. There are so many questions that I need answer to. Why people in the Karoline's block and what were are the names of the people that were killed?

My daydreaming almost made me to pass the turn to the meeting point. Sharply, I hit the brake and cars behind me just barely avoided a massive collision. I turn to right and park the car by the little bistro on Canada Avenue. Gina is already there and surprisingly she is accompanied by Leah. Gina waves at me to come but I am unable to move. Why Leah is here and where is Kenny? What if this is some kind of trap to get her again incriminated into something that she is not involved in? So far I did not have a chance to share with Gina my findings regarding Kenny and even though she knew that clues are very strongly pointing at him I cannot predict what he might have told her in order to convince her about his innocence. There is a strong knock at the car window next to me.

'What are you doing? Come out I need to talk to you and don't have lots of time,' Gina seems very anxious and looks around her all the time. That makes me feel more at ease. Now I know she is still on my side. Why otherwise she would be worried about who is going to see her talking to me? I get out of the car and make sure that my face is as expressionless as possible.

'Why is she here?' I ask quickly.

Leah is not looking at me. Also her look seems to dramatically change. She is wearing the old jeans and brown t-shirt that I believe must be older than me.

'Leah has something that she needs to tell you.' Leah is pushed by Gina towards me. I am very curious about the incident that happened at Karoline's place but somehow I don't think I should interrupted the monologue that Leah is about to give me. Leah is still fidgeting when Gina smack her shoulder.

'Ok. Don't push me, I will tell her.'

Leah finally looks up and there are many things that can be read from her expression. There is lots of fear, sadness and most of all guilt. Her make-up is smashed almost everywhere around her face.

'I just want to say that Kenny had nothing to do with what happened.'

'What actually happened, Gina?' I am getting tired of waiting for her. I still need to know what Marshall find out about Ralph and this meeting is becoming too long for my comfort. Leah takes a deep breath and continues.

'I found out that he was cheating so I just needed to make sure that she understands that he is mine. I mean she had the chance with him before he met me. They knew each other for a long time but noooooo, she had to become interested in him once he was committed to me. I am tired of always letting people get away with it. Why everybody always want to take from me what is mine?' I am looking at Leah trying to comprehend what the hell she is going on about but without success. I turn my head towards Gina making sure that my expression will give evidence of confusion.

'Stop talking around it and tell her,' Gina yells at Leah.

'I only wanted to scare her. I didn't know it was going to get out of hand and that she would start fighting me. I had no other choice than to protect myself. It was accident. She started pulling my hair and calling me names so I grabbed the first thing that I found and hit her over the head. On the way down she hit her head again and I think that killed her but I am not sure about it. The only thing I remember after is me panicking. I was worried that Suzy might walk in and see what happened.'

The moment she mentions Suzy's name my mind become dark. I know she is still talking but the words are not reaching my ears. Karoline is dead. She is dead because again she gave priority to herself instead of thinking about her child. She was always as selfish as our mother. Maybe it is because they spend so much time together while I was fighting to become successful detective and achieve something that is meaningful in my life. How could she think that life with mobster will be without risk? And what the hell was Kenny thinking getting involved with my sister?

'So you killed my sister?' I am aware she said it but I feel like I need to hear it one more time.

'Yes, I did but I didn't mean to. Afterwards, I wanted to get rid of her body but neighbour saw me and I panicked so I got rid of him too.'

Leah is now shaking her head looking everywhere around her crazily. I would love to hate her for what she just told me but the sight of her struggling with her guilt and realisation that she will never get out of it without going to prison for rest of her life makes me feel sorry for her. The girl only wanted somebody to love her and give her the home that she always wanted but instead of that she wound up with men that only used her and kick her out. First time she wanted to stand up for herself and it ended up with the disaster.

'Gina, what happened today at Karoline's place? Why Kevin said that there are three people that were killed in the incident?

'The three people are Karoline, a neighbour and Kenny. He was killed during the arrest by Kevin.'

This is all just a nightmare but without the relief of waking up. Leah is still shaking her head and the moment Kenny's name is mentioned she starts sobbing.

'I cannot believe that my love is dead. I only wanted him to help me move the body. I tried to put lots of ice around them in the bath but they were starting to smell so I had to act quickly. I called Kenny to help me but he didn't know what I had done. But he still came. He still loved me and wanted to be with me. '

Leah's behaviour is becoming more and more irrational. She is moving up and down the street and getting unwanted attention from passer-by. We are not too far away from the station and we cannot afford somebody getting suspicious.

'Leah calm down. Yes, Kenny loved you.'

My reinforcement of her belief made her calmer and more stable. Inside I was worried though. I should be more upset that Leah killed my sister but instead I am furious at my sister. This didn't have to happen if she at least for once listened to me and stayed away from Kenny. Prior my conviction I did talk to her and tell her that in order for her not to be in danger I need to continue pretending that I am quality. I even told her about Kenny and my request to care for her and Suzy but I also warned her about Kenny's profession. As always that didn't stop her from getting involved again with wrong person just like first time when she got involve with Jack, a drug addict that completely fucked up my life because he was at the wrong place at the wrong time.

'That is not all, Kate. But firstly I would like to apologise for doubting you. I went with Kevin to snoop around your place thinking we might find something. Of course he didn't know that I was already there and that it is actually Karoline's place. After we discovered Karoline's body in the neighbour bathroom Kevin automatically assumed that it is you. So now everybody thinks that you are dead.'

Oh now everything make sense. That is why Kevin was excited about giving statement to the press. Now he is finally going to become hero that he always wanted to be. He is the one that solve two homicides and most possibly catch the serial killer that was running the streets...ME...

'Don't sweat it Gina. Take her back before Kevin become suspicious. Will call you later.' It is time to finally end all this and maybe this time my sister might be the one to do the sacrifice here instead of me.

Chapter 34

It only took me couple of minutes and I was back with Marshall preparing for our next step. However, this time everything is different. I feel lonely and full of regrets that might be unjustified. I know that I am not responsible for what happened to Karoline. Every action has its own consequences and she knew it. I look at Marshall at the driver seat and see him getting ready for the fight that will change everything and it makes me wonder if I am not doing the same thing as Karoline and risking it all for one man. Kenny was no different to Marshall. They both work hard to fit in it. The most important connection that they had though was their love for their women, love for their family and their need to protect their family.

'Are you ready to finish it all?' Marshall asks me as he hands me a gun.

'I am ready to put a dot after all of this.' My response fits the situation. There is nothing to finish anymore but some closure is definitely required. This time there will be no more continuity and loose ends.

I get out of the car followed by Marshall. There are another six to seven cars parked behind us and the owners of vehicles start following us towards the empty warehouse. The chilly sea air is all around us as we make our way towards our destination. Marshall told me that this is the place that Ralph wanted to meet him at, so it means this is the place that he was supposed to find his resting place. Ralph doesn't expect that I am going to be coming as well with a handful of people that are still loyal to Marshall. Ralph will look at it as fight for turf and great opportunity to get everybody on his side by winning. Hopefully, his arrogance will be as high as always as that would suit my plan immensely.

The other side of the warehouse situated outside of the San Jose is used as a storage facility. Many drug dealers use this place for trading and other illegal activities. I let Gina know that the last fight will take place here. The place was suggested by Ralph but he doesn't realise that it is perfect place to solve all our problems without endangering anybody else. I didn't hear from Gina confirming that she received my message which is unnerving but understandable. She cannot have anything linking me to her especially now when everybody from the law enforcement thinks that I am dead. I am sure that they are on the way here. Kevin would not want to miss such a great chance to become bigger hero than he is already in the eyes of his co-workers. I can clearly imagine his expression as Gina told him that there is a meet up here with potential successor of Marshall and his gang. I haven't heard anything on the news from Kevin, which means he delayed his statement that would reveal Kenny as serial killer and me as one of his victim. No, he wants to add the arrest of underworld boss under his belt before that.

We are being followed by the Marshall's people as we turn the corner besides the factory. On the other side of the street is Ralph and his men are awaiting our arrival. The closer we get mobsters become more nervous and keep reaching for their guns. The rules are rules though and they still need to wait for the orders. There is no reason for the blood if they do come to some kind of understanding.

'Well, well, well. I always knew that you had a weak spot for this, little traitor.' Ralph didn't even look at me as he said it to Marshall.

'I am standing right here Ralph. Would be nice if you acknowledged me before you start trashing my name.' Ralph is getting more annoyed with me, which suits me well. I don't want this gathering to become very peaceful anyway. I need them to know that I am here to fight and I will fight as strongly as needed in order to win this war.

'I thought that you are past your crime time, Ralph and here you are trying to take over.'

'Well somebody has to! Otherwise you would take it all and that is something that I will never allow. A little bitch police whore is not going to take what is rightfully ours.' His voice became louder. He takes the gun from his case and everybody follows his lead.

'What about you Marshall? And all the others behind you? Are you really willing to die for the person that is working against you? She is the opposite of what we are and one day she will destroy you. Think before you act! There is no need for blood shed here. Not between the family!!!' Ralph is now more in the centre of it all. It reminds me of the motivational talk that I heard from the cult leaders years ago during my first years in police department. It made me see that there are two types of people: leaders and followers. Leaders definitely know how to use the gift of words and use it to manipulate the ones that are weaker. I can see that Ralph would be one of them. Who knows? Maybe if he wasn't the mobster he would be a politician.

'So what do you suggest that we do now?' Marshall asked as he also takes out the gun.

'The time for spring cleaning has come and it is time to take out the trash. We will never be what we used to if we allow her to remain between us.' Ralph came closer to Marshal and is ready to negotiate. Mobsters are wary and look around ready for any kind of movements from the other group. Suddenly I feel buzzing in my jean pocket and know what it means. Gina is here and now it is my time to give them the sign.

Chapter 35

'IT IS ALL A TRICK!' I scream and look up towards the warehouse window.

Everybody is following my gaze and they all pointed out the gun towards the window. I fire three shots towards the sky. I think this is enough of the sign for Gina. I start running towards the main door as the shooting starts.

'You bitch!' Ralph screams and starts firing all his ammunition at me. I manage to run through it all but as I am about to enter the building some of the bullets hits the window and glass starts flying in all direction. One piece of the glass deeply pierces my leg. I am still able to run but it takes lots of my power to keep my speed. I know that the moment I fall it is all over. I can feel the blood flowing out from my wound and I feel dizzy. I look back and see that Ralph is now getting closer to me. I turn towards the closest door and start running even faster.

'Just run little rat. But you cannot win,' I can hear his laughter and the chill spread around my body.

As I close the door to one of the storage door Ralph starts banging on the door but after couple of seconds there is quiet. Well, not completely quite. You can still hear people shooting outside. I slightly open the door and peak out. I see police officers all around. Kevin and Gina just came in with more men. Marshall is just up the stairs and I think it is Ralph that he is running after which would explain why he stopped following me.

Kevin sees Marshall and starts chasing him instead to the second floor of the building. Gina looks in my direction and makes a gesture with her hand that implies that I should leave. I close the door and look around. The building seems to be from the 17th century, very old, dusted and full of cracks. In the corner of the room is another door. I go there and slowly open them. There are stairs that lead upstairs. I know that I am in no condition to fight but I have to go and make sure that Marshall is ok.

'There is no bloody way!' I hear a scream and look back down at Kevin who just came out of nowhere. The other scream must belong to Ralph who is now fighting with Marshall on the third floor of the building. We both look up and see Ralph upper body handing out of the stairs and Marshall above him crushing his leg. I use Kevin slip of concentration and start running. I hide around the corner of what must be the meeting place of mobsters. There are two leather sofas in the middle of the room and many beer cans on the floor. Kevin is right behind me and aims his gun at every little corner that he sees. I know that he knows that I am there listening.

'I always knew that you can cheat death but wow this is a bit creepy.'

Kevin looks at the corner near the door expecting to find me but I already moved to different area of the room. I am still too far from the door and there is no way I will get there without some major confrontation that I might not survive.

'I see some blood,' Kevin laughs and wipes his

forehead with the back of his hand in the dramatic way. 'So you are not immortal after all. For a second I got worried.'

Kevin looks behind the couch when he hears noise outside of the main door. Slowly he walks to it with his gun aiming straight at the middle of the door. This is my chance. I slowly start to follow behind him and just as I am about to strike him Marshall appear at the door. He knocks Kevin down and they start to struggle on the floor. I am trying my best to get a clear shot but without success. There is a huge risk that I will injure Marshall by mistake. Plus at this point I am sweating and my vision has been compromised.

Kevin gets back his balance and stand up followed by Marshal. They both now don't have any weapon so they fight with their bare hands. Marshall sees me with gun and quickly disarms me by kicking me in the leg that is wounded. I cry in the pain and get on my knees.

'Finally you are where you belong. On your knees crying.' Marshall runs to help me but is stopped by a kick to his stomach. The blow's force him to take couple of steps back. I can see in his face that he is exhausted and cannot hold up any longer. He looks at me as Kevin starts punching and kicking him furiously. The final blow to the back of his head sends him flying out of the huge factory's window that was behind him.

'No!!!!' I scream loudly. This is not how it was supposed to end.

Chapter 36

The pain is no longer important. Everything that I have ever loved is gone and now there is only vengeance. I stagger to my feet with the gun in my hand. I point it at Kevin and take a shot but with my blurry vision and shaking hand I had no chance. Kevin is right in front of me now and with a childish slap on my wrist he pushes the gun out of my hands. Kevin throws me against the wall and drags me by my shirt and hair towards the window.

'If you care about him so much maybe you should follow in his footsteps.' I fall to my knees and I can see Marshall's body on the ground. We are both surprise when we see that he is still moving but as most of the officers are on the other side of the building there is nobody to help him. On the other right side of the building I see a person that is running towards the parked cars. I am about to yell for him to help Marshall but as the person turns back I see that it is Ralph who is escaping.

'Another two ungrateful punks who know how to cheat death. The chase is becoming really tiring.' Kevin turns his back to me and walks to pick up the gun on the floor. While I was on the floor I felt something under me. Pieces of the glass are everywhere. I picked up the biggest one I could find and use the last amount of power that I have to rush to him before he can get hold of the weapon. The edge of the glass is forced inside of his left hip. Kevin screams in pain. He looks at me with the eyes that don't have any emotion. This moment confirmed something that I was suspecting for a long time. This fight is no longer about revenge for him. The whole time he was trying to show he is hero by killing bad people but in the process he lost something that he can never get back: his humanity. Now he is one of them. We both keep staring at each other and the last couple of years before I went undercover flash in front of me. The gun is now in my hand but I am struggling to pull the trigger.

'Don't try to justify it Kate. You know that if you don't do it I will be back for you and for your whole family that is still alive. It is your fault. You destroyed me years ago when you betrayed me and now all these people are dead. Their blood is on your hands.' Kevin holds his wounds and with a smile he slides down the wall, leaving the mark of blood behind him.

'No you are wrong. What I did was for the right reasons. What you did was purely for your need to gain as much power as possible.' I don't want to do it but this is my only way. I can see in his eyes that if I don't finish it now he will be back and I am not willing to lose any more people I love.

#

Gina barges inside the room as I pull the trigger. She must have heard me screaming as Marshall fell out the window. I lower the gun and take a closer step to Kevin. This time I will not make any mistake. I pull trigger another two times just to make sure that he will not cheat the death

'You shot him,' Gina says in disbelief. I know that from her point of view it looks as I killed him without giving him chance. I became the judge, jury and punisher.

'No I didn't. Remember I am already dead.'

There is a noise as police officers start rushing back to the building. I believe most of the mobsters were already arrested or they flew the premises.

'Listen to me, Gina. He killed Harry, your brother. He was walking the street of our home and killing anybody that stood in his way.' I take Gina's hand and move closer to her to make sure that I have her attention. 'You really think that he would stop. We don't' have anything that we could use against him in the court. In the eyes of the people he would always be the one that killed Kenny that was named as a serial killer that public was scared of.'

'Ok. But what should I say now. Why is he dead?' Gina asks me with such an innocent voice that it makes me gently hug her.

'Don't worry. Just say that he was dead by the time you got her and blame it on Ralph. I will take the gun and discard it.'

Gina is still standing in disbelief and shock but there is no more time to waste.

'I have to go and help Marshall. He is injured on the other side of the building so give me a bit of time before you send your men there. Don't worry it will be all right. Ralph will take over the whole organisation and believe me he will be mad and ready to kill. You need to make sure that he will be stopped.'

Gina opens the door slightly.

'It is still clear but they are close so don't go by main stairs. Be careful.' Gina pushes me out and instead of going to the left where are main door I start slowly running the opposite direction and towards Marshall.

Chapter 37

Dalena is standing by the body of her daughter. Her face is full of despair as a mortician pulls the sheet from the Karoline's face.

'Oh my god! My daughter!' Dalena starts crying.

'Ms Summers, this is important. Can you please confirm with me the identity of this person?'

This is a crucial moment for them to close the whole investigation. The head of the police department is waiting outside for the confirmation of what they already know in order for them to give the statement to the public. Kate Summers, an ex-detective, who played fundamental role in catching many members of underworld world, is dead. Furthermore, it will finally be announced that Kevin died in the line of duty while he was trying to apprehend the new underworld boss Ralph who is currently awaiting his trial. Everything fell into place and nobody is suspecting that Kate is still out there. Unfortunately, Kevin will not be able to face the justice and take responsibility for his action and therefore it will have to remain Kenny who is going to be viewed as the killer of mobsters.

'Yes, this is my daughter Kate.' Dalena is still crying as Gina takes her to the next room and ask her to wait for her outside by the car.

Gina goes outside and announces to her co-workers and new department boss that Dalena Summers confirmed the identity of the deceased person as that of her daughter Kate Summers. Afterwards, Gina goes back to her car where Dalena is waiting for her.

'So do you know where she is?'

'Yes, I do. We should go and pick up Suzy now. Kate has to leave the city before anybody sees her wondering the streets.' Gina takes the turn right towards Hilton hotel where Dalena and her granddaughter are staying in.

#

I get out of the car and take a deep breath while Marshall is waiting outside. This is it. The new beginning that I was hoping for but this time I will not let anybody to screw it up for me. The second car enters that car park and stop just next to me. Gina and Dalena get out of the car but Suzy is nowhere to be seen.

'Where is she?' I am on the edge now. I don't know if Suzy will believe that I am her mother. After all, I am no longer Kate but Karoline and there is no point to tell Suzy otherwise. At least not yet.

'She is in the car. I just thought maybe we can talk before you go away.' Dalena always knew how to surprise me.

'I don't have time for this now. Just say what you want to say.' I am in no way interested but at least I can give her a slight benefit of the doubt even though she never gave it to me. I do love my mother and in some sick way she did made me be a person that knows how to be independent, confident and determinant but she never gave me the mother's love that I needed. She never looked at me with the eyes of somebody who cares and wants to be part of my life so I don't see the reason why I should start now.

'Suzy needs a mother. I finally understand it and I understand you. I wasn't the best mother and I can see it now. Suzy has a chance to have normal life. Karoline was never there for her and was doing the same mistakes as I was doing in the past. You don't know how many time I had to take Suzy to live with me. Karoline was on the rocky path and now when you are finally off yours I know you will take care of her.'

I cannot believe my ears and eyes. Dalena has finally taken some responsibility and there are tears in her eyes. Maybe there is still chance even for us.

'I will mother. Don't worry this is not the end. I will be in touch and you will see your granddaughter again'. I hug her as she starts crying.

'Mummy!' I hear the scream behind me and as I turn Suzy run towards me and hug me with all her power.

'I missed you. Where were you?' Suzy asks me but it is difficult for me to reply as I am worried that I will start crying.

'I had to take care of something but from now on we will be always together.' I kiss her cheek. She is so beautiful. Her hair is darker than mine or Karoline's and her eyes are colour of the brightest sky. She is holding a little teddy bear in her hand and with the other she is holding me trying to reassure herself that I am really here.

'You promise.'

'I promise, little one.' I slowly take her to the car where Marshall wait for us and put her at the back seat.

'So this is goodbye?' Gina asks me worryingly. I will miss this little fiery girl but I am sure this is not the end. I am sure I will hear a lot about her in the future.

'No, Gina this is the beginning of something new and I am sure we will meet again. Take care of yourself.' I hug her strongly. She will one day become great detective and I am proud to say that I was part of that journey. At least she got something out of this mess. His brother is dead but she was promoted and now has a chance to make even bigger difference in the world. I smile at her and at my mum who is still crying.

'Bye.' I get in the car and look back at Suzy.

'You ready to go?' I ask her and with a big smile she gives me a nod.

'Yes, we are ready.' Marshall takes my hand and kisses the back of it. The family was created today and I will make sure nothing will divide us again. It took some time for Marshall to recover from his injury but he managed to get through. Words were exchange and finally I said the words that he was waiting to hear for a long time, 'I love you'.

'Wait.' Dalena knocks on the car window and I can see she is holding something. I open the door and she passes me a little Yorkshire terrier dog. I completely forgot that Suzy has a dog. I love dogs but this is too much for one day.

'She will not be able to fall asleep without him. You will thank me one day.' I cannot help the angry grin as I take the little fella. I pass the dog to Suzy, who is now happier than before.

'Mummy what does it mean?' The word mummy will be something that I will have to get use to but I love it more every time I heard it from her mouth. I look at her and see she is pointing at my left foot where I have my tattoo.

'It means justice.'

Marshall smiles at me and slowly moves the car into the outgoing traffic. At the end I was unable to save my sister but maybe I can do a better job at being her.

The End

Author's Profile

Born in the Poprad and educated in Slovakia and England, Kate has a solid background in the media and business as an actress, producer and PA. After four years of working in the film industry, Kate decided to finally fulfil her dream of writing a book based on the action script belonging to her and her business partner's company, Challenging production

(www.challengingproduction.com).

Currently, Kate is finishing her psychology degree at Derby University and working on her second book THE BEAUTY OF BELONGING following the story of soldier that falls in love with a German woman during World War II.

Lightning Source UK Ltd.
Milton Keynes UK
UKOW02f2101190515

251877UK00002B/5/P

9 781785 072918